The Long Arm of Tull Clancy

Johnny Hornet Series
Book One

Henry Helbog

Door Number Three Publications

I

Contents

Foreword

This new novel from Henry Helbog was a pleasure to read and review. Henry has created a character who could easily become a reader's favorite. Why don't you settle down and enjoy a fine Western written by one of the great new names in the Western genre.

You will not regret it.

~ *Robert Hanlon, author of the* Timber: United States Marshal *series and many others.*

Chapter One

"**C**ome right in, sir. I'm Mrs. Brockbane. May I offer you a drink?"

The stranger followed the woman into the front parlor of her social club. "Thank you, no, ma'am," he said, removing his hat.

She gestured to a red divan edged with carved mahogany. "Won't you be seated?"

When she was not looking, the young man's eyes scanned everything in sight, missing nothing. The open doorway leading to a flight of back-stairs was of particular interest to him.

"I'm sure it hardly warrants mentioning, sir, but I wish to inform you that this is a first-rate establishment, meaning that we don't allow any manhandling of the girls." Mrs. Brockbane paused as she looked at him. "That is, unless the client pays an additional sum and pledges to restrict his excesses."

The stranger looked back, his gaze level. "I'm not

here to hurt anyone." He took his seat.

There was a momentary pause, as though the statement was not what she had expected. "Ah, I'm delighted to hear that. I knew you for a gentleman the moment I laid eyes on you." The proprietress sat down in the armchair across from him. "May I ask your name, sir?"

"Caldwell. Theodore... Caldwell." The proprietress did not miss how unpracticed the visitor sounded using the name.

"You're a stranger in town, are you?"

"That's right."

If the proprietress thought she would get more out of her question than that, she was mistaken. "I see. And might I inquire as to what sort of lady you have in mind for the evening?"

"A natural blonde would suit me, and eyes of blue."

"Well, you're in luck, sir. We have a French girl who's new to the territory and our establishment. Hardly speaks a word of English, but she's well versed in the art of pleasing a man." She paused to wink. "She plays two different musical instruments and has a singing voice to match her rare beauty. Of course, she'll cost you a little more than the others, but she's well worth it."

The stranger shook his head. "No, I'm not sure she'll do. Have you any other blondes?"

"As a matter of fact, I might have just the girl for you. She's known as a bit of a wildcat. Not quite broken in, but perhaps she would fit your requirements."

"She might be the one for me. Would you call her down for me to look at?" The stranger tried to sound disinterested, but he was in the presence of a shrewd woman who missed nothing and could as often as not read the minds of her clients like a book.

"Why, Mr. Caldwell. You haven't asked a word about her appearance. I can't think when the last time a client of mine wasn't interested in what one of my girls looked like."

He nearly fell into the trap of chuckling and feigning amusement like any simpering cow-hand caught in a dissemination. Instead, he assumed a cold expression. "I haven't said I would take her yet. Show her to me, and then I'll decide."

Mrs. Brockbane reached up casually to tug twice on a velvet bell-rope. As she stood up, she gestured to the doorway leading to the stairs. "I think you'll find just what you're looking for beyond this doorway."

The stranger stepped toward the open doorway. Before he could pass through it, however, an immense man, with broad shoulders and cruel, deep-set eyes, blocked his way.

Noting the confused look on the stranger's face, the proprietress chuckled. "Do you think we're stupid, Mr. Hornet? That's right; I'm well aware of who you are. I guessed your identity almost as soon as I laid eyes on you."

"How the devil would you know who I am?"

"I was forewarned by Mr. Clancy that you might show up someday, and your resemblance to my Miss Hattie marks you out as her brother."

"If my sister's up there, then you'd better let me pass. You have no right to keep her here against her will."

"Tull Clancy is the law and authority in this town. That gives me, acting under his instructions, the right to keep her here for as long as he wants her to serve her penance."

"Penance? You can't be serious. She hasn't done a

damn thing to deserve being here."

"Oh, but she has," said Mrs. Brockbane with a sneer. "She defied the Clancys by refusing to wed Mr. Clancy's oldest boy, William. It was her insult to their honor that put her here."

"How ironic that you or any of the Clancys should speak of honor."

"Go home, boy, before you find yourself in a world of hurt. You're not to come here again."

Hornet put his hat back on and lowered his head. He let out a long breath as though in weary resignation, and began to turn away.

One moment Hornet was a study in slow lethargy. The next, he sprang into action. Planting his left foot, he swung and connected with the lantern jaw of the bordello guard. Long days of pent-up frustration at being unable to find his sister lay behind the punch. The guard, his face ugly with anger and contempt, staggered back on his heels. Before he could respond, Hornet drove his fist into the pit of his stomach.

The guard hardly seemed to feel it. With a challenging roar, he surged forward to send a heavy fist toward Hornet's face. The young man dodged the blow, but not fast enough. Hairy knuckles clipped him along the jawline, opening a bloody gash.

"Hit him! Hit him harder!" cried the proprietress. "Teach him a lesson!"

Encouraged by his employer, the guard pressed his advantage by relentlessly flailing his long arms at Hornet like a whip, driving Hornet further into the parlor as the younger man sought to keep out of his reach.

Himself spurred on by an inner rage at the injustice suffered by his sister, Hornet got in a quick jab to his opponent's eye. Momentarily dazed, the brute stepped back to shake off the blow for a second. Hornet didn't give him that second to recover. He aimed a deliberate blow to his nose, transforming it into a bloody pulp. This was followed by an uppercut to the brow that started a stream of blood when he connected with his ring.

The brute staggered further back. Half-blinded by the blood that had been unleashed, he held the other arm outstretched. This left his right side unprotected. A stinging blow to the temple there was followed by further jabs to the mouth and neck.

"Fool!" hissed the proprietress. "He's making a laughingstock out of you. He's hardly more than a boy."

Far more used to fighting drunken ploughmen, the brute had already come to the end of his endurance. One final haymaker put him on the floor, where he crumpled into a bulky heap.

Hornet stood triumphant over him, heaving great gasps of air. The proprietress meanwhile stood appalled, unable to believe her own eyes. The brute had never failed her before.

Hornet rushed up the stairs to the landing. Before him was a narrow corridor with three doors on each side and one at the end. "Hattie! Hattie! Are you up here?"

From behind one of the doors was a voice. "John? John? Oh, God— is that you, John?" Thank God you've come."

"Where are you, Hattie? Hurry and come out."

"I can't. My door's locked from the outside. I'm behind the third door on your right."

"Stand back," he said before throwing his weight against the door. The timber began to splinter, but the lock held.

Two female heads, alerted by the noise, appeared momentarily in two of the doorways. One glanced at Hornet with a lascivious smile. Their curiosity satisfied, both disappeared again behind their respective doors.

Again Hornet brought his shoulder to bear against the door, this time getting through.

There were tears from both brother and sister as they clasped each other in their arms. "You're almost safe now, Hattie. I've come to take you away. Hurry and get dressed," he said, noticing that she wore only a satin chemise.

"I'll just be a moment, John." Within three minutes she had packed her few meager positions in a valise and wrapped a shawl around her shoulders.

"Quickly," he urged as they hurried down the stairs, each step sounding a creak.

They had just passed the brute, who still lay motionless on the floor, when they saw Mrs. Brockbane standing by the only window set in the side wall of the parlor. She was holding a double-barreled Derringer that she had withdrawn from her bodice.

"That's far enough," said Mrs. Brockbane. "Hattie, get back upstairs. You're not going anywhere."

"I've come too far to be stopped now," said Hornet, waving his sister to stand behind him, out of the line of fire.

"This gun begs to differ."

"I'm unarmed. I left my sidearm with my horse. Kill me now, and it'll be murder— and, I'm sure, bad for business."

"I don't need to kill you unless you force me to, boy. Not when I can simply shout for help out this window. Some of Mr. Clancy's ranch hands will be just down the street in the nearest saloons and within earshot. Then I'll just hold you here at gunpoint until they arrive."

As the proprietress spoke, Hornet felt a nudge from his sister behind his back. In the next moment, she passed him something glazed and hollow, probably made of porcelain. He suddenly remembered that there had been a small statuette of Cupid on the corner table to the left of the doorjamb behind them.

"I have money. Give us a chance to pay our way out of this," he said, stalling for time as he planned his throw. He would have to hit the hand that held the Derringer or the gun itself dead-on. Nothing else would do. A hit just above or below would likely result in the discharge of a bullet finding its way to him. In his younger days he recalled pitching balls at targets at a local fairground, and twice he won a prize. There would be no time to wind up and take careful aim at this target, however.

"Ha," sneered Mrs. Brockbane.

As he had hoped, she began to tilt her head toward the open window so as to project her voice when she called for help. In that instant of her eyes shifting from them, he acted. Just as she inhaled to shout, he whipped the object at her. It struck as intended. The gun went off, but the shot was forced low, passing through a small Oriental carpet and embedding itself in a wooden plank on the floor beneath it.

Before the stunned proprietress could recover her wits and raise her gun for a second shot, Hornet was upon her, twisting it out of her hand. The weapon clattered onto the floor, the second of two bullets unspent.

Mrs. Brockbane struggled free of Hornet's grip and, breathing heavily, staggered to the window sill. Griping the sill, she shrieked into the night. "Help! Help! Murder!

Every Clancy man, come to my aid at the social club! Help! Help!"

Just as she took in a fresh breath to shout again, another figurine, this time gripped by Hattie, came crashing down on the proprietress' head, sending her unconscious to the floor.

"Come on," urged her brother, slipping the Derringer into the pocket of his jacket. "We've only got moments to get away."

They made for the front door but stopped short in the entryway. Hornet cursed under his breath at what he saw through the lace curtains. Two of Clancy's ranch hands, who happened to have been passing by when Mrs. Brockbane cried out for help, were starting for the door.

Hornet slid the door's bolt into its groove. "We'll have to find some other way to get out. Is there a back or side door?" he asked.

"Yes, there's a side door leading to an alley and a back door as well."

"Let's try the side door."

However, as they approached the door, they heard voices just beyond it, followed by a pounding. "Damnation. Our luck seems to be running out. Let's try the back door."

They were confronted with the same problem at the back door. There, a group of men were beginning to break down the door.

"There's a balcony outside Mrs. Brockbane's room upstairs," said Hattie. "We could try climbing down one of the support beams under it while those men are busy at the doors."

"Good thinking. Let's try that."

Just as they passed the apparently inert body of

the guard, however, the wounded man, groping with an unsteady hand, seized Hornet's ankle from behind. Hornet fell heavily to the floor, where he rolled onto his back as the brute climbed over him and sought his throat. The guard's face was so bloody and numb with pain that he didn't seem to feel the new blows that Hornet rained down on him. On the verge of blacking out from being choked, Hornet remembered the Derringer. Extracting it, he clubbed his opponent's skull three times until the brute's thick, square-tipped fingers finally went slack.

Hornet gasped for breath.

"We've got to hurry, John, up the staircase— quick," urged Hattie as she helped him to his feet.

Despite Hattie's support, her brother swayed drunkenly as they scrambled up the stairs. Halfway up, he stumbled badly before righting himself. Once beyond the landing, they hurried down the corridor. Finally reaching Mrs. Brockbane's empty room at the end of the corridor, the siblings burst into it. Once in, they slammed the door shut behind them.

Just as they heard men surging in through the back door, the pair clambered over the railing of the balcony. "Now's our chance to get away," said Hornet as they shimmied down the post, receiving more than one splinter for their effort. "They're all inside the house now."

"They're upstairs! They went upstairs again!" screeched Mrs. Brockbane, who had just come to and was staggering toward the foot of the stairs. "I just heard them go up."

"Fine," said Hornet, alighting on the ground and reaching up to help his sister down. "This actually helps us. Let them all go up and search the rooms. With luck, we'll get to my horse and be away before they've caught sight of us."

As luck would have it, however, the first room that Mrs. Brockbane searched was her own. They heard another outraged screech as she spotted them from the balcony while they ran pell-mell across the vacant lot behind the building.

The first of Clancy's men poured onto the balcony just as the brother and sister reached the horse tethered at the mouth of the nearest alley that ran between two houses. They managed to get off three or four rounds, sending chips of clapboard flying, before the couple were too far out of sight further down the alley.

Mrs. Brockbane's voice rose high in accusation and venom. "You won't get far with that girl! Do you hear me? Clancy's men will hunt you down and you'll pay for what you did! Both of you will pay dearly!"

Chapter Two

Tull Clancy sat in his wheelchair looking out the broad set of windows in his upstairs study. No one outside of his immediate family and personal doctor had seen him since his riding accident; nor would they until he had fully recovered. A reputation built on strength, fortitude and pride could not, it was thought, be shown in any other light.

One wall of his study was lined with books on conquerors, military tactics and the histories of crowned heads and emperors. On another could be seen framed maps, Indian lances and shields, animal hides and a collection of European and American swords and firearms spanning three centuries until the present day. The pride of his collection was a sword that had once belonged to the "Napoleon of the West," Santa Anna. Displayed in a glass case, its pommel was encrusted with a golden eagle, its grip made of shark skin entwined by gold wire and the cross-guard decorated with a lion's head.

When he looked out his windows at his dominion, Clancy saw thousands of acres of prime cattle land stretching to the horizon. His was one of the richest and most prosperous spreads in the county.

There was a knock on the door downstairs. A servant let in the foreman, Jake Malloy, who was there to see William Clancy, the oldest son of Tull Clancy. Dismissing the servant, Clancy spoke to his foreman in the reception hall.

"Bad news, sir."

"What is it, Jake?"

"Hattie Hornet has escaped from Mrs. Brockbane's. Her brother found her and broke her out. Some of the boys and me started to track them but lost them in the darkness of the wooded slopes outside town. I've come to ask for further instructions."

Clancy cursed. "Wait here, Jake. I'll go up and report this to my father."

"I presume he's not going to be happy about this one bit."

"You're right about that. This isn't the news I want to bring him," he said before heading up the wide, semi-circular staircase.

William Clancy had learned to fear his father from an early age. Along with that fear had also come a strong desire to earn his respect. Even now, today, as he entered his father's study, he could feel those old impulses follow him in like a loyal hound.

Ten minutes later, William came back downstairs. "Well, Jake. As expected, he's fit to be tied. He says for you to take a dozen of your best men and ride out after them in the morning. Don't come back till you've found them, or have a good excuse for not finding them."

"We'll be up at the crack of dawn. I have an idea where they might have gone."

"You know what's at stake, don't you? We can't have Hornets on the loose poking their noses around at such a delicate time."

The foreman nodded with understanding. "We'll get them."

◆ ◆ ◆

No longer hearing the sounds of pursuit, John Hornet slowed his horse to a walk. They soon found the stream they'd been looking for that ran north. Entering it, they slogged through the bed for a good five miles to hide their tracks, then angled away from it.

He and his sister had been lucky, riding headlong in the dark in the first frantic moments without running into a rabbit hole or tripping over a rock or root. Above them, the stars shone through a thin film of cloud. The air was cool and crisp. Each breath they took was like downing a cool drink. Hattie clutched her shawl closer to her throat.

"Well?" said Hornet to his sister behind him in the saddle. "Aren't you at least going to condemn me for taking so long to find you?"

"I've nothing to condemn you for, John. I know you'd have found me sooner if it were possible."

"You always were too patient and tolerant for your own good." He bit his lip, wondering if, under the circumstances, he'd said the wrong thing and had just added to her misery.

"Now I'm just tired. Old and tired."

"Old? You're barely twenty-one."

"Yet I feel as though I've lived for years and years and that my life is almost at an end."

"There's where you're wrong, Hattie. You couldn't be more wrong. Life, from here on, will be what you make it. You can start over again. You can go somewhere new where no one knows you and never look back."

Her silence was like a knife drawn across his cheek.

Minutes passed before she finally spoke again. "How did you find me?"

"Someone tipped me off —left me an anonymous message under my door at the hotel when I passed a night there."

"I'm glad he did, whoever he was."

"When you disappeared four weeks back from Mrs. Tullie's boarding house, most people were of the opinion you had run off."

"You had another notion?"

"Yes. First of all, you're not the running-away type. Also, I found the timing strange, coming so close on the heels of your refusal to wed William Clancy."

"I loved him. I really did love him at one time. That's the irony of it," said Hattie in a soft yet bitter undertone. "We'd grown up together; there always seemed to be an inevitability to our marrying, long before it was even spoken of openly. It just happened that it was also what Dad and Mr. Clancy had always expected and wanted of us."

John nodded. "And it would have bound our two ranches together."

"But William changed. He changed in a thousand subtle ways, just like his father before him. There's a streak of cruelty in both of them. I could never have loved him for what he'd become. What they did to me just confirmed my suspicions."

"I'll take you away from here, Hattie. I'll take you far, far away— to somewhere no one's ever heard of Tull Clancy and his brood."

"But can you take away the name from my mind?"

"Hattie—"

"Don't you see? No matter how far away I go, I'll always be pursued by my memories."

"Memories can die, like anything else— eventually."

To this she said nothing. It seemed at that moment that they'd never been farther apart.

◆ ◆ ◆

It was dark as pitch when John and Hattie came within sight of their destination. The stars, now behind a thick veil of clouds, gave no light to see by.

"Where are we?" asked Hattie, who'd been dozing in the saddle and unaware of her surroundings.

"We're finally coming up on the Graysons' farmstead just ahead. I thought we might spend what remains of the night here before moving on."

Hornet, dismounting, helped Hattie down from the saddle before tying his sorrel to a stud-ring embedded in a cottonwood. Next, he got the saddle off and left it in the grass. That done, he knocked on the door, prompting a furious barking from somewhere within the house. A minute later, when light bloomed in the front room, they heard the sounds of someone tramping heavily across the floorboards. The light intensified. The footsteps came to an abrupt halt. "Who's there? What do you want?" said a voice on the other side of the door.

"It's John. John Hornet. I've got Hattie with me."

The door was flung aside by a thick-set man dressed in long flannel underwear struggling to hold back a dog by the collar. It was Bill Grayson. At Grayson's feet was a shotgun and lantern that had just been set down.

Before Grayson could speak, his wife, Margaret Grayson, appeared alongside him. "Hattie Hornet! As I live and breathe! Is it really you, Hattie?"

Exhaustion mixed with relief led Hattie to collapse into the waiting arms of Mrs. Grayson.

The sun was barely more than a sliver above the horizon when twelve men, grim and stern-faced, rode out from the Clancy ranch. They had been given a task to perform, and it did not occur to them to question the rights or wrongs of it. When Tull Clancy branded someone an enemy, that person became their enemy as much as his.

An hour later, they picked up the trail of the two

fugitives just outside town. The hoof prints eventually descended into a stream, which they followed northward along its bank.

"What lies in this direction?" asked Jake Malloy.

"A scattering of farmsteads and settlers," replied Crosby, a gaunt, pock-marked man at his side.

"Then that's where we're headed. We'll make a thorough search of each of them."

"What about the old abandoned Hornet ranch home?"

"Unlikely they'd go there. Nevertheless, if they don't turn up soon, we can swing by there later on."

It was mid-morning when four of the twelve, having split from the others to make a sweep of the farms west of the stream, topped a rise.

"What's that ahead of us?"

Crosby lowered his hat brim against the morning sun. "It's the Grayson farmhouse."

◆ ◆ ◆

John and Hattie, sitting alone at the kitchen table, had just started on their morning meal.

"Oh— before I forget," said Hornet, sliding Mrs. Brockbane's Derringer across the table's oil cloth toward his sister. "Take this and keep it with you at all times."

"What would I need that for?"

"You never know. There might come a time when

I'm not around to defend you. Think of it as a weapon of last resort."

Hattie, shrugging her shoulder, picked up the unfamiliar weapon and put it away in her reticule that lay on the table.

"I spoke with Mr. Grayson before he went out to feed his stock this morning," said Hornet. "He's offered to lend us a horse so we can each ride our own."

"Bless him for that and for sheltering us overnight."

"Soon as we've finished eating and he gets back, we'd best be on our way."

"Where can we go?"

"The Graysons think that the safest place to be is among the sodbusters and sheepherders who live down in the lower valley. They're the natural enemies of the Clancys. Over the years they've had no end of disputes with the Clancys over access to water holes and livestock straying over boundary lines in both directions."

"I've heard about those flare-ups from time to time. But we don't know anybody from there well enough to stay with."

"No, but the Graysons do. They've got close kin there and have offered to take us to them when Mr. Grayson comes in."

"That's great, but will we be safe there from the long arm of Tull Clancy?"

"I think so. We'll be staying where there's a cluster of houses, each but one or two brimming with large families who know how to handle their long guns and protect what's theirs. Even the Clancys daren't go buzzing around there."

"That sounds marvelous."

Hornet skimmed a biscuit across the gravy on his plate, and spoke again. "By the way, how are you feeling—now, today, I mean?"

"I feel a sense of relief that I'm out of harm's way, or almost."

"I can't understand how they could have done what they did to you, simply for refusing to marry William."

"I believe there's more behind it than a punishment for bruising their egos."

"How do you mean?"

"Do you remember Dad speaking about a hidden cache of gold and how both the Clancys and our family were each supposed to be in possession of half a map leading to it?"

"Well, yes, but I've never quite been sure if that was really true or not. I thought maybe that was just a joke of Dad's."

"No. I think that the two maps as well as the gold do actually exist. I overheard William and his brother, Edward, make repeated references to the maps and cache when I was at their ranch house."

"You were there?"

"Yes, but only for a few days. Then I was taken to — to that place you found me."

"What did you hear them say about it?"

"I could only hear snippets of conversation through the wall of the room I was in, but it was enough to know that they're making efforts to get at it."

"But without our half of the map, there's no way they could find it. If it ever really did exist, I think it would have been destroyed in that fire that killed Dad six weeks ago."

"To hear them, you'd think they already had both halves, or else are close to getting our half." She paused and looked intensely into her brother's eyes. "Johnny, don't you think it's possible that that fire was no accident and that Dad was killed for his half of the map?"

Hornet, his lips tightening into a grimace, stared down at the last of his uneaten eggs and skillet potatoes. "I don't think it's hard to suspect, despite the conclusions of the marshal's investigation, that something wasn't right about Dad's death."

Hattie's eyes welled with tears as she thought of her father.

"What I wouldn't mind doing is to try hunting up one or both of those maps and beating the Clancys to the cache, assuming it's not too late."

"But where would you even begin to look?"

"I don't know. Maybe at the Clancy ranch house."

"But surely—"

Just then, dogs began barking. "Hattie, stay in the bedroom, would you, until I'm sure all's well?"

"You don't think they've already found us, do you?"

"No, but let me make sure." Hornet, his hand on his holstered revolver, made his way to the kitchen window and leaned out. About a hundred yards distant and headed toward the house was Bill Grayson, his two dogs circling him. They'd just rounded the henhouse and were abreast of the hog pens.

Just as Hornet lifted his hand in greeting, he felt the hard press of cold metal against the side of his head. "Reach!" said a gruff voice.

While he raised his hands, a second person —Jake Malloy— from his other side plucked Hornet's gun from its holster and slipped it into his own waistband. Then, coming into view behind Grayson, he saw two horsemen riding at a walk, each cradling a rifle, as they herded the farmer toward the house.

"I'm sorry," said the farmer when he reached Hornet. "They took me by surprise. There wasn't anything I could do."

Hornet nodded. "Don't worry about it, Mr. Grayson."

"I thought about shouting a warning to alert you, but they'd already come up close enough to drop me if I had. Maybe I should anyway have risked it."

"Forget it."

Malloy motioned with his gun for Hornet to back up into the kitchen. The window being low, he slipped over the sill while still training his gun on Hornet. Two other gunnies followed Malloy in through the window. One remained behind to watch over the horses and the farmer.

Malloy tipped his hat back. "Where's your sister, Johnny?"

"In a place of safety— far away from here. You won't be seeing her again, and neither will that scum Clancy that you work for."

Malloy slashed Hornet across the shoulder with the barrel of his gun, sending him sprawling against the tabletop.

"Search the house," said Malloy, putting his gun away as Hornet rolled off the table onto the floor. A few moments later, he began to slowly rise.

A door at the other end of the kitchen opened. Mrs. Grayson appeared. "Johnny? I heard voices. Is Bill back from—" She stopped short when she saw the gunmen and then Hornet, one hand braced against the table and the other covering his wounded shoulder.

The foreman doffed his hat. "Sorry for the intrusion, ma'am. This won't take long. We've come for the Hornet girl. Once we have her, we'll be out of your hair and on our way."

Standing just inside the nearby bedroom behind the half-open door was Hattie, who'd frozen in panic. Hattie hardly listened to what was being said as she stood rooted to the spot, moments away from discovery. Uppermost on her mind was the unfairness of being so soon caught. She shuddered as she thought of what would happen to her and to her brother.

"Is she in there?" said one of the gunmen, gesturing over Mrs. Grayson's left shoulder with the barrel of his gun. She turned to look in the direction indicated. From her angle she caught a glimpse of Hattie beyond the door adjacent to the one she had come in through. Their eyes met for a fraction of a second.

"How nice!" said Mrs. Grayson, angling a step nearer the gunmen but actually positioning herself so that her back could more clearly be viewed by Hattie.

"Huh?"

"How nice," she repeated, scowling. "Here I am in my own home, and here you are, completely uninvited and pointing a gun at me. I'm not even armed, and you're threatening me with deadly violence." As she spoke, Mrs. Grayson's hand dropped behind her back, to where her apron strings were tied. There was a gesture— a gesture meant only for Hattie's eyes. Mrs. Grayson was pointing — no, stabbing— with a single finger at the floor.

Hattie came out of her trance and stared at the finger motioning downward. What could Mrs. Grayson mean by this? Then it dawned on her. Hattie glanced down at her feet and then, pivoting, looked behind where she stood. There was a throw rug, faded and threadbare and covering a small section of the floor in front of the window off to the left. Could it be? Hattie trod softly toward it and drew aside the rug. Beneath it was a trapdoor, leading, no doubt, to the root cellar. With a heave, she opened it. There was a ladder leading down into a realm of darkness. Would she have time enough to make her way down the ladder before the gunmen were in the room?

Mrs. Grayson, bless her, seemed to be doing her best to distract and delay her enemies.

"Step aside. I'm not going to ask you again," said the gunman.

He brushed past her and pushed open the door. His eyes scanned the room. It appeared to be empty. Luckily for Hattie, his eyes did not immediately look down at the floor, or else he'd have noticed the final movements of Hattie's slender hand stretched out across the floor to reposition the rug as best she could. A second later, the hand, along with all other traces of Hattie, had vanished from the room as the trap door closed into place. Even her valise and reticule were gone.

The gunman's eyes, perhaps attracted to the uneven rug, focused on the floor and narrowed. He was in the process of reaching out for the upended corner of the rug with his foot, perhaps to uncover it, when his attention was diverted by a movement over by the window. Mrs. Grayson, who had entered the room after him, was drawing shut the drapes in the window and turning her back to it.

"What are you doing there? Move away from that window."

Mrs. Grayson, breathing a sigh of relief, complied.

The gunman took a quick step toward the window. "What have we here? Is there something you didn't want me to see?" He threw open the drapes and peered out the window across the pasture and the woods that lay beyond it.

"You find her in there?" said Malloy, appearing in the doorway.

"No, but I've a fair idea of where to look for her."

Chapter Three

The sun was still shy of noontime when the party of gunmen returned to Tull Clancy's cattle ranch, known as the Triangle X. Hornet, his hands tied to his saddle horn, was being led on his own mount by the foremost rider.

William Clancy stood waiting out by the hitch-post in front of the main house, a riding crop gripped behind his back. Before him, offering shade for the house, was a grove of six cottonwoods. His eyes momentarily scanned the faces of the riders before settling on Hornet.

"Welcome to the Triangle X," he drawled. "It's been a long time, Johnny. Don't think I've laid eyes on you in over a year or two."

Hornet glared at him. "You go to hell, Clancy. Go to hell for what you did to my sister and for everything else you've done in your wicked life."

Clancy chuckled. "You always was a firebrand, Johnny."

"And your old man can go to hell too."

Clancy's smile faded to a scowl. For a long while he didn't speak. When he did, it was in a quiet and menacing tone. "You're not to speak that way about my father, especially not here, where he's within listening range. Apologize."

Hornet was about to continue in the same vein, but something told him that he might put his life in jeopardy if he did. "All right."

"All right what?"

"I'll play it your way. You hold all the cards— for the moment." He gritted his teeth. "So take my apology, for what it's worth."

Clancy said nothing for a minute. Perhaps he was weighing in his mind whether the apology was sufficient. "Get him down off that horse and into the house," he said to his gunmen, flicking his crop as he spoke. Turning, he passed through the doorway ahead of them.

Malloy and one of the gunmen helped Hornet down from his horse, after which they led him into the house. The other hands led their horses and Hornet's mount into the nearby barn.

"This way," said the foreman. "It won't do to keep the Clancys waiting." Chuckling, he closed the door behind them.

◆ ◆ ◆

The trapdoor, pulled up by an unseen hand, thudded onto the floorboards.

26

Hattie, looking up, feared the worst until she noticed the smiling face of Mrs. Grayson. When she reached the top of the ladder, Hattie saw the inert form of one of the gunmen sprawled across the floor in the doorway. "Oh, God! Is he dead?"

"No. Just stunned. I got him with my skillet when his back was turned. Luckily he was the only one they left behind when they went off through the woods looking for you. He won't worry you none now; he'll be out cold for a long while to come."

After Hattie had passed up her valise and climbed out of the hole, Mrs. Grayson closed the trapdoor and replaced the rug. "Do you think they'll be back again?" asked Hattie.

"Sure enough, but not for a while yet."

"The others that were here— they took John away?"

"Yes, Hattie. I'm sorry."

There was the sudden sound of a wagon approaching.

"Don't worry," said Mrs. Grayson, noticing the agitation that it caused Hattie. "It's only Bill bringing the buckboard round to the front of the house."

"The buckboard?"

"It's so he can transport the gunman into town and place him in the custody of the marshal. Personally, I don't think that marshal's good for much. He's more than likely to just turn him loose, seeing as how he seems to be close to Clancy. But we've talked it over and can't think of anything else to do with him."

"What about me? Do I go back in the root cellar when they think to come back here again? I wonder if I couldn't have a candle with me next time, as it's awful dark down there."

"No, no. Absolutely not. As soon as Bill comes back, we'll load up the wagon and all of us will head out to the valley to his kinfolk. We're all better off if we hole up for a while where the Clancys can't get at us."

"Oh. John mentioned that he'd spoken about the valley to Mr. Grayson."

"You'll be safe and sound there."

"I'm awful sorry we got you involved in this and that you have to leave your home. I feel just terrible for you and Mr. Grayson."

"It's the Clancys you should blame, not yourself. We'll be all right. Maybe Bill and I will be able to return in a couple of weeks. We're too old for them to stay mad at for long and to bother with."

"I don't want to be a burden on anybody, especially your relations, who are strangers to me."

"No matter who we are in life, we're all strangers to each other until we meet for the first time. I'm sure you'll get along just fine with them. They've got eight children, so one more at the eating table won't inconvenience anyone. And as for being a burden, I wouldn't look at it that way and neither would they. If you're willing to work hard, there'll be plenty of chores you can do to help out. Right now you need to be around people and you need to do other things to keep your mind off what you've been through."

"I don't know how I can ever repay you."

"Live and be happy again. That's the only payment I could want."

"You're a good soul, Mrs. Grayson," said Hattie, holding back a tear. "I almost feel like I don't deserve such kindness."

"Don't ever say that, Hattie. That's about the most foolish thing you could ever say."

Mr. Grayson came in just then. After tying up the gunman's hands, the three of them carried him out to the back of the buckboard. They covered him with a tarpaulin in case anyone from the Clancy ranch should happen to pass the wagon on its way into town. When Mr. Grayson drove off, the two women went back into the house with the dogs to wait for his return.

Two hours later, Mr. Grayson was back. After loading up the buckboard with their dogs and various belongings, the three of them climbed up onto the spring seat. Heading south and then east along an old cattle trail, where the chances of running into a Clancy rider were less likely, they proceeded toward the valley that would be Hattie's home for the foreseeable future.

Hornet sat in an armchair in the Clancy-family drawing room. His hands, still bound together, were in his lap. Standing at the door behind him were two gunhands, their arms akimbo.

"Are you comfortable?" asked William Clancy from the couch opposite his chair. Between them was a low, circular hardwood table imported from India, its four supports carved into the shapes of elephant heads along the table's edge and their trunks stretching to the floor and serving as table legs.

"I'm more comfortable now than I've been these past several days."

"Oh?" said Clancy, his voice feigning interest as he opened his cigarette case and selected a cigarette. "Why is that?"

"Been sleeping under the open sky a lot lately."

Clancy held out his open cigarette case, and his visitor took one. Clancy lit Hornet's cigarette and then his own. "In a gallant quest for your sister."

"That's right."

"A sister that belongs to me."

"Not now she doesn't."

"Well, we'll see about that."

Hornet said nothing in reply.

"Do you know that I loved her? Ever since I was a child I loved her."

Hattie had said almost the same thing, thought Hornet to himself. "You have a queer way of showing it."

"I don't have to explain myself to you. Nonetheless, I take solace in knowing that whatever happened to her, she brought it on herself."

"Say that to yourself all you like, but we both know it isn't true."

Clancy, frowning, turned over two of the glasses on the table and began pouring wine into the nearest glass. He paused with the decanter poised over the second glass. There was a hard flick of the eyes to his guest. "Drink?"

"Sure."

Clancy poured. "Ever been up against a copperhead?"

"Once or twice."

Clancy handed Hornet his glass. Hornet, holding it

in both hands, lifted it to his lips.

"Then you'll know that they can strike suddenly, without warning, especially if you step too close to them."

At the end of his statement Clancy sprang up to drive his fist into the pit of Hornet's stomach. Hornet's drink fell from his hands and shattered on the wood floor. The wind forced out of him, Hornet keeled over onto the floor.

Clancy stood over him as his enemy coughed and spluttered on his hands and knees. It was some minutes before he recovered. Hornet glared up at him as he reseated himself.

"That was a vile and cowardly thing to do, Clancy, though not nearly as vile as what you did to Hattie."

Clancy, seated again, leaned back in his seat. His eyes dropped lazily, as if suddenly bored. "Where's your sister, Johnny?"

"Haven't you abused her enough? What do you want with her anyway?"

"I'll ask one more time: where is she?"

Receiving no answer, Clancy nodded to his two gunhands.

In his mind's eye, Hornet saw himself rise to his feet and charge into Clancy with all his weight and hatred and pummel his sneering face to a bloody pulp in the seconds before the two gunhands could reach him.

But it was not to be. He still hadn't fully recovered from Clancy's unexpected attack when they reached him. It was agony to be set upon before the wind was fully back in him. Once again he found himself on the floor. In response to the merciless barrage of kicks and punches, he could do little more than curl up into an undignified ball and cover his head with his arms. His only thought was to survive the beating so as to exact revenge at the first available opportunity.

Six or seven times he was asked by Clancy where his sister was, and each time he received the same answer: "I'll kill you someday, Clancy! I'll kill you!"

Hornet's body eventually went limp. There was no longer any reaction— no quivering or recoiling— to any of the blows. Blood ran freely from gashes to his head and face.

"That's enough for now," said Clancy just as the boot of one of his men was poised to land on the unprotected head of Hornet. "Looks as though he's senseless."

"What you want done with him now?" asked one of the henchmen, breathing heavily after his work-out.

"Can't do much of anything with him now, till he wakes up. The Hornets always were too pig-headed for their own good. Hmm," muttered Clancy in contemplation as he stroked the waxed end of his moustache. He went over to a nearby writing-desk and, with his dip pen, scratched out a couple of lines on a sheet of paper. After folding it twice, he added a name in block letters on the outside, then handed it to one of the gunhands. "Sid, go into town quick as you can and give this message to the name you see. Don't let anyone else see it. You're to hand it directly to him."

Sid Varden put his hat on and departed for the stall where he kept his horse.

The other man jerked a thumb at Hornet on the floor. "And what about him? Should we just leave him where he is?"

"No. Take him outside to the nearest corral gate.

I'm not done with Hornet yet. I've still got plans for him."

Chapter Four

The noonday sun was in Hornet's eyes when he awoke to find himself propped up against a corral fence, his back lashed to the rails. His shirt was off and he was hatless.

Hornet was in a sorry state. It seemed that every joint and muscle in his body cried out for relief. His vision swam and his thoughts seemed to be in a jumble.

"Hornet," said a voice.

He tried to focus on the blurred face in front of him. Perspiration ran in rivulets down his forehead. He blinked several times and shook his head to clear it. Finally the face began to come into focus. It was the face of Clancy's foreman, Malloy.

"Water. Gimme some water."

Someone came with a dipperful of water and passed it to Malloy.

"This what you want?"

Hornet, lifting his head, nodded.

Malloy drew back the dipper to fling the contents into Hornet's face. Already raucous laughter could be heard coming from four or five hands looking on.

"No," said a voice that he recognized as belonging to William Clancy. "Give him a sip for just a second—enough to leave him with a hankering for more."

When this was done, Hornet ran his tongue along the stubble around his mouth and drew in what little moisture there was. The droplets of water there and the small amount he had sipped from the dipper did little to slake his thirst but were welcome nonetheless.

"You can have all the water you want, Johnny, soon as you tell us what you're going to tell us," said Clancy as he exhaled smoke from a cigarette.

"To hell you go, lowlife vermin," spat Hornet.

"That's not a satisfactory answer. Not by a long shot."

"You won't get any better answer than that. I'd die before I'd tell you where she is."

"Then it's time we put you to the test." Clancy turned to his foreman. "Jake, see if you can offer our distinguished guest further inducement to cooperate."

Hornet noticed for the first time that a coiled-up bull-whip hung from Malloy's belt. Malloy loosened the braided leather and cracked it against a barrel once or twice for effect. He then sprang nimbly over the corral fence behind where Hornet stood tied to the rails.

Four times the whip lashed his back and four times Hornet winced but did not cry out. Malloy would never get off a fifth lash.

"That's enough!" said a harsh, commanding voice. "Turn him loose."

All eyes turned to the sight of the local deputy

marshal, Tom Dugan, his eyes blazing and his mouth set with grim determination.

"Who we have here?" said Clancy, his eyes falling on the badge sparkling in the sun. "You the new deputy marshal?"

"That's right."

"Where's Marshal Briscot?"

"He ain't here. I am."

"Maybe you'd better go talk to Marshal Briscot. Him and us got an understanding. We got—"

"I don't know what kind of understanding you may have and maybe I don't want to know, but with me it's not the same, understand? So why don't you just turn this man loose like I asked?"

Clancy scowled and bit his lower lip. He looked as though he'd impart harsh words. Instead, when he next spoke he took on a friendly tone. "Why don't you just step inside the house a minute so I can explain matters to you."

"I don't think so, Mr. Clancy."

Clancy flicked away his cigarette with casual indifference. "A little time is needed. Then you're bound to see our side of things."

"We'll see about that," said Dugan in an obstinate tone that warmed Hornet to him. "But at the moment, I see only a victimized man being unlawfully whipped."

"It's not without good cause," replied Clancy as if explaining to a child.

Despite the appearance of the deputy, Malloy still held his bull-whip aloft and looked poised to continue using it. The deputy turned to the foreman. "That's enough! I said to drop that." The deputy drew his revolver and leveled it at Malloy, who reluctantly cast the bull-whip aside.

The deputy reholstered his gun and strode purposefully forward. Stepping between Hornet and the deputy was Clancy. "No serious or lasting harm was done to him, Deputy. I'd appreciate if you'd forget about this."

The deputy snorted. Reaching Hornet, he untied him and then fetched a dipperful of water.

Hornet drank long and deep. Afterwards, he lumbered painfully to the nearby pump, the deputy following. There Hornet refilled the dipper and poured it over his head. The water washing over his body felt like heaven. "I'm glad you came in time, Deputy."

"So am I, son. You well enough to ride into town with me? I'd like a full statement from you. Also, the office might be the safest place for you at the moment if you'd like to stay a night or two. I can all but guarantee your safety for as long as you're there. Or, there's always the hotel across the street from the office."

Hornet got into his shirt and buttoned it. His jacket followed. "Fine with me, Deputy. Right now, anywhere but here is a good place for me," he said as he rubbed his sore wrists.

Dugan handed Hornet his hat, which he clapped on his head. "I think we might have a salve back at the office to help with your wrists and back, by the way."

"Sounds good to me."

Under protection of the deputy at his side, Hornet reached his horse and started to lead it away. With the deputy's own horse in tow, they walked abreast. Hornet suddenly remembered something. "My gun belt."

"Where's his gun belt?" said Dugan in the direction of Clancy and his foreman.

Someone brought it out and threw it at the

deputy's feet.

"Better watch out for him, Deputy. Boy's in a hot-headed state," said Clancy; "so I don't doubt he could do us some mischief, either now or later on when he might come sneaking back in the dark."

Dugan looked from Clancy to Hornet. "Not that I'm taking any orders from Clancy, but, all things considered, I think I'll hold on to your gun for now, Hornet, so as to avoid inciting any of them." Without waiting for a response, he rolled up the belt and holster and slipped it into one of his own saddle bags.

There were black looks from the gunmen and Clancy in particular as they threaded their way past them, but nobody made any effort to hinder Hornet and the deputy. Once beyond them, the two men mounted their horses and rode off.

It was not until they were passing through the outer gate that Hornet felt at ease. "I want to thank you again for helping me get out of there, Deputy."

"Think nothing of it, as it was my duty. You mind telling me what that was all about?"

"It's a long story."

"So I take it you didn't just steal one of their heifers or something like that and earned yourself a whipping as punishment?"

"No. Far from it. If anything, the reverse is true, though far more extreme than the theft of just a heifer."

"I see. I think I'd like to hear more about this. Just what did they take from you then?"

"They took my sister— carried her off against her will a month ago. It wasn't till today that I managed to free her."

"You mean they kidnapped her?"

"They sure did —only it was far worse than that."

"Is it something you're able to tell me about?" prompted the deputy.

"I don't know whether I should or shouldn't, because what's done is in the past, and people like the Clancys never suffer for their crimes anyhow, no matter how heinous. And, above all, Tull Clancy's reach is long."

"If I'm to help you, then I'd like to get all the facts at hand. Wouldn't you like to at least try to press charges for what they did?"

"Maybe you don't know it yet, but people who try to go up against the Clancys have a nasty habit of ending up dead or just short of it. It's a fact that Tull Clancy owns just about every mining concern, gaming house, saloon and important mercantile establishment for a hundred miles in every direction. Going up against him is like trying to ride through the teeth of a sand storm. It's a tall chore."

"You don't strike me as the type to roll over."

"I'm not, but I know what I'm up against. I know for a fact they control all the levers of power in this town — and that includes, I'm sorry to say, the law officers such as the marshal you work under."

"And I'm even sorrier to hear you say that. But just because the marshal has been compromised doesn't mean I have."

There was an interval of silence, during which Hornet seemed lost in thought, or perhaps was weighing the unpalatable thought of telling all or else maintaining a silence for the sake of family dignity.

Having reached the entrance to the canyon that lay midway between the Triangle X and the town, the two riders stopped at the edge of the stream that meandered along the canyon floor. After letting their horses have their fill of water, they made their way to the west sidewall and the narrow ledge that sloped up along the wall before eventually spilling out onto the open prairie beyond.

The ledge was narrow and, in places, treacherous, so they led their horses by their reins up the incline on foot, the deputy marshal going first, followed by Hornet.

"That sister of yours," said Dugan over his shoulder; "she safe somewhere?"

"I think so. I hope so."

"You know where she is?"

"Not exactly at the moment," he said, thinking, as did Malloy and his gunmen, that she'd fled through the Graysons' window. Since she hadn't been brought back to the Triangle X, he assumed she must still be in hiding in the woods or else already back at the Graysons' farmhouse by this time. "But I think I can find her. I can only speak to the general vicinity."

"Wouldn't you like to fetch Hattie with us on the way back to the marshal's office? Then we can take you both into protective custody."

"Say, how is it you know her name?"

"Don't know. Guess I heard it somewhere— maybe back at that ranch. So how about my suggestion?"

Hornet's eyes narrowed as he looked at the deputy's back. A suspicion began to stir in him. "I already told you: that marshal you're working for is not to be trusted. I don't know that she'd be safe there—or myself either, when it comes to it."

"And I've already told you that I'll guarantee your safety. I can say the same for your sister."

"How can you guarantee our safety or anyone else's

so long as the marshal is in charge?"

"I think you may be judging the marshal too harshly; but how about the following. You and your sister can bed down at my house. You can lay low there for as long as you need to. My missus and daughter will be happy to accommodate you. We can sneak you in the back way. How does that strike you?"

"Thank you, but I don't think so."

"Why not?"

"Because I think maybe you could be in league with them."

"With the marshal?"

"Him and Clancy. Yes. I got a notion you are."

The deputy chuckled. "Your notion is plain wrong, mister. I hardly know the marshal; I've only been on the job a week; and I never heard of Clancy till today."

"So, not enough time to be corrupted is what you're trying to get me to believe."

"I'm not trying to get you to believe anything."

"Tell me something. How is it you happened to turn up at the Clancy ranch today?"

"Why, it was the marshal's idea I should come out to make myself known to the Clancys. I'm doing the same for all the bigger ranches and farmsteads."

"Why didn't he come with you, to show you the way and to introduce you to people?"

The deputy grimaced. "What is this? You interrogating me?"

"No, but I think I've got you pegged."

Dugan was about to respond, when Hornet, slipping past the deputy's horse, eased the lawman's gun out of his holster. Dugan turned to see the muzzle of his own gun pointed at him. "Up with your hands, Deputy.

You can let your horse go up ahead a ways."

Dugan, glowering, said nothing for the moment; then he spoke. "You're making an awful mistake, Hornet."

"Yeah? I don't know about that. You going to get your hands up?"

Dugan raised them. "Son, I don't think you know what you're doing."

"I know enough by now to know I can't trust anyone. That includes you."

As instructed, Dugan stood aside with his back pressed against the cliff wall so his horse could pass him, prompted by a slap on the rump from Hornet. After about thirty yards on its own, the horse stopped, looked back and decided to wait where it was for its owner.

"What now?" asked Dugan. "You intend to shoot me in cold blood?"

"For the moment, I intend only on getting your wrists into those handcuffs of yours." As he spoke Hornet reached for the cuffs that hung from the deputy's belt.

"'Fraid I can't let you do that." Dugan, clapping a proprietary hand to the handcuffs at his side, squared his shoulders and lifted his chin as he looked with calm resolve into Hornet's eyes. "Give me the gun," he said, reaching for it.

Hornet backed away. "Don't be a fool, Deputy."

Dugan, acting as though he was gripped by madness, continued toward Hornet.

In the second before Dugan could reach him, Hornet lowered the gun from his adversary's chest to his leg, and pulled the trigger. He regretted being forced into firing a shot but was content to wound rather than kill.

The trigger fell on an empty chamber. He squeezed it a second time even as he took another step back and bumped into the muzzle of his horse. Again there was no discharge. Instant realization came to him that the deputy had deliberately been carrying an empty gun as a precaution against Hornet using it against him. He again saw Tull Clancy's hand in the foresight.

By this time, the deputy had closed on Hornet, landing a stinging blow against the side of his head. Dazed, Hornet stumbled back against the shoulder of his horse. His horse tossed its head once and backed away.

Pressing his advantage, Dugan swung again, this time putting everything he had behind a haymaker that would knock Hornet out. But Lady Luck was against him. At the very moment Dugan would have connected, Hornet, tripping on a rock, fell heavily onto his back.

The momentum of the deputy's swing, unchecked, sent him toward the cliff edge. There, for what were only scant seconds but seemed an age to the lawman, he danced an absurd-looking step all along the brink, sending scree that had accumulated on the ledge sliding down the thirty-foot sheer drop. More by chance than agility, he eventually managed to find solid footing again.

Hornet, on his backside shaking the cobwebs out of his head, was just in the act of getting to his feet, when Dugan lashed out with a kick. The kick, however, inflicted no damage, as Hornet had enough presence of mind to block it with his hand.

Frustrated by this, the increasingly incensed deputy then launched himself on Hornet. With one hand clutching Hornet by the throat, the lawman wound up his fist for another punch as he crouched over him. But he never connected. Hornet, with the deputy's gun still in his right hand, brought it crashing against the side of Dugan's head.

Dugan, stunned and losing consciousness, rolled from Hornet and headed for the cliff edge. His body hung along the edge in mortal peril and was about to tumble over.

With no time to lose, Hornet dove onto his stomach toward the deputy and grabbed hold of his shoulder and shell belt. However, the lawman, now unconscious, continued to slide over the edge as he broke loose from Hornet's grip, with the dead weight of his legs the first part of him to go over.

Finally, Hornet was left with only a hold of the deputy's arms as the rest of his body hung slack over the edge. The arms, too, began to slide from his grip until he was left holding him only by the wrists. Hornet's own body began to slide as well, pulled by the weight of the other.

"Wake up! Wake up, damn you! I can't hold you much longer."

Hornet's arms were going numb. In a matter of seconds he would be unable to hold on any longer.

Deputy Marshal Tom Dugan was about to meet his Maker, and there was nothing Hornet could do to prevent it.

Chapter Five

"Wake up! Wake up!" bellowed Hornet one last time.

Just at the point when Hornet would have to give way to the inevitable, the deputy's eyes shot open.

"Climb up! Climb up! Quick!"

Dugan, blinking, glanced about and realized the extreme danger he was in. Inch by inch, he was slipping through Hornet's hands. Hesitating no longer, he took a firm hold of Hornet's right hand, then placed his other hand upon the ledge. Slowly he pulled himself up and, with Hornet's help, up over the edge to safety.

Both men lay panting on their backs for some minutes, the deputy relieved that he was still alive after his narrow escape and Hornet glad that he had been able to save a life.

Dugan sat up and felt his head. His hand came away wet with blood, so he wiped it off with his bandana, then used that same bandana to tie around his head. Picking up his fallen hat that lay close at hand, he put it on and leaned back against the inner cliff wall of the ledge. Under Hornet's watchful gaze, the deputy fished in his shirt pocket for his makings to build a smoke. "Cigarette?"

Hornet nodded.

Once he'd rolled the first cigarette, the lawman handed it to the younger man, then started on the next. Striking a match against the limestone wall, he lit Hornet's cigarette and then his own. Both men noticed the trembling of his hand, but neither remarked on it.

Dugan shifted his body to make himself more comfortable, then tipped his hat brim lower against the sun. "That was a close shave," he remarked.

"I suppose it was."

The deputy took a long drag on his cigarette. "You didn't have to save me."

"No, I didn't."

"How come you did, especially after I lied through my teeth to you and strung you along for an ill purpose?"

"Why does anybody do anything?"

"'Tain't no answer."

"Well, then, I guess it was a spur-of-the-moment decision on my part. I saw a fellow rider in need of help before he fell to his death, so I helped him. Saving you doesn't mean I like you, Deputy. You're as bad as the marshal and some of the others under the influence or in the pay of Clancy. Maybe that offends you, but that's how I see it."

The deputy chuckled. "I don't mind. What you say is true enough. Mind you, I did feel fully justified in deceiving you at the time."

"Justified? How do you mean?"

"They told me you'd been a nuisance to them the last few months, getting into drunken brawls with some of their hands in town and holding on to the odd cow of theirs that strayed onto your grazing land. And I was also advised that I should discount anything you said about a kidnapped sister, that it was all made up to smear the Clancy name."

Hornet laughed a bitter laugh.

Dugan studied Hornet's face. "You mean none of that was true?"

"I don't hardly see how it could be, since I just came back to these parts last week after being away for eight months. And as for my sister, every word I've told you about her and more besides is true. It's them that's lying."

"I'll be damned." The lawman reflected. "Of course, you could be lying."

"I could."

"But you're not," he observed pointedly.

Dugan, having finished his cigarette, stood up to brush the dust off the length of his body. He stepped to the cliff edge and looked down into the gorge for a long while, perhaps to imagine where his broken body might have been lying at this moment.

"What now?" asked Hornet.

"Now?" The deputy turned to meet the younger man's gaze. "Now is where I offer you my profoundest apology for playing you false all along. Also, for being dim-witted and gullible enough to be taken in by the Clancys and that corrupt marshal I work under. I could also add 'pig-headed' to my faults."

"You could, but since I don't hold any grudges, I wouldn't worry overly about it. It takes a true man to admit when he's been wrong."

"Anyway, I want you to know that you've earned a devoted friend for life on this day, and here's my hand on it."

Hornet stood up to shake the lawman's hand. "Well, I can use all the friends I can get, since I know how powerful the forces are that are aligned against me."

"You want some advice? Clear out. Get as far away from here as possible, taking your sister with you. You can never win against the likes of Tull Clancy. No one can."

"Some things are worth fighting for."

"Maybe so, but not in this case."

"You sound sure of the way things are stacked for someone new to town."

"I've seen and heard a lot in the short time I've been here."

"Do you know anything about a cache of gold or a map to it? I've reason to believe that getting at the gold is their ultimate aim, though the kidnapping of my sister is related to it." Hornet explained everything he knew.

"Well, now that you mention it, I have had the impression something big was in the works, without really knowing what it was. Tell you what. If anyone ever confides something relevant to me about this, I'll contrive of a way to get the information to you."

"That could be of great help. You know the big oak tree at the crossroads just east of town?"

"Sure."

"If you have a message for me, you can leave it in the hollow of that tree. I'll check for something there every so often — say, once a day, if I can manage it."

"All right."

"What will you do now?"

"Think I'll continue on into town. I'll show the marshal the bump on my head and tell him you caught on to my act and got away."

"I'll be obliged for that— though I don't suppose either the marshal or Clancy will be none too pleased to hear what you have to report."

"No, but what I'll say to them won't be too far from the truth. I'll only be altering the ending of my tale a little. And yourself? Where are you headed?"

Hornet hesitated.

The deputy held up a palm. "Come to think of it, you shouldn't ought to tell me, and maybe it's better I don't know."

"As a matter of fact, I don't see the harm in telling you. I'm going into town same as you. The only difference is that I'll wait in the outskirts till nightfall to avoid being spotted by one of Clancy's men or the marshal."

"What business have you in town?"

"Oh, maybe none, but it's possible there could be some answers to some questions I have in town. What I'd like to do is sniff around, maybe talk to one or two persons of interest."

"Well, I guess there's no use in me trying to talk you out of it, so I won't, but I wish you all the luck in the world, since I think you're going to need it considering all that you're up against."

They parted company just before the crossroads.

Hornet watched the deputy head down the road leading into town, then led his horse into a thicket, where he tethered it to a thick root and loosened the cinch.

It was well after dark when Hornet started on the road into town on foot.

On two occasions travelers heading out of town came toward him. Each time he melted into the shadow-rich trees along the road until they had passed. A couple of muleteers were the first to pass, as harmless as they were intoxicated. The second group that passed —three cowmen— were from the Clancy ranch. It would be three fewer potential enemies to worry about.

It was possible that by now the word was out that he had escaped from the deputy. However, there was presumably no reason to suppose that any of his enemies would think he had any business in town. Nonetheless, it was with watchful, darting eyes that Hornet proceeded past the first of the shacks and sod houses lining the approach into town. Once closer to the town center, he kept to the shadows of the back lanes.

Hornet had a notion that Clancy's freight-haulage office might be a good place to start his search for information. But getting into the office undetected, even in the dead of night, wouldn't be easy. Even at this late hour there were revelers out and about. Most were idling outside saloons or bordellos in the main drag or else sauntering afoot. Every so often he heard the shuffling of someone making his way down one of the alleys in his direction, but they were easily avoided by stepping into a side passage until they had passed.

Clancy's office was in the main drag, putting Hornet at risk of being seen were he to try entering from the front. Instead, he made his slow, cautious way up a northerly alleyway that would eventually connect with the alley that ran east to west behind the building housing the office.

Hornet was almost at the juncture that led to the back alley and was about to turn into it, when three shadow-clad figures coming from the main drag suddenly loomed at the mouth of the alleyway before him. The foremost was a shorter, slighter figure, while the two others just behind were immense. Fortunately for Hornet, the nearest gas-lamp in the main drag, which would otherwise have illuminated his face, was broken. Being cloaked by the darkness gave him a measure of comfort. Despite that darkness, Hornet nonetheless caught the glint of steel that denoted a firearm in the hand of one of the bulky figures.

"Aha! There you are!" said the foremost person, jabbing a finger at his chest. The voice was gleeful and triumphant. "Now you'll get what's coming to you!"

It was Mrs. Brockbane, the proprietress from the bordello.

Chapter Six

Stunned at the seemingly chance encounter that had brought him face to face with Mrs. Brockbane and confronting the prospect of being returned to Clancy's ranch to face the wrath of his enemies or even killed outright now where he stood, Hornet could think of nothing to say.

"What's the matter, low-life? Cat got your tongue? You've got just ten seconds to pay up what you owe me."

A confused Hornet blinked. "Pay up? What are you talking about?"

"Wait a minute. Who are you?" Hornet felt a fumbling hand groping the contours of his face in the dark. "You're not Josh Radcliff."

Hornet's best guess was that a client —the aforementioned Josh Radcliff— had run off from her brothel without paying what he owed.

"Let me light a match to be sure it's not him," suggested one of her henchmen. There was every chance that either he or the other bulky figure was the same man Hornet had already tangled with in the bordello. If so, that would put his life in imminent danger, if it wasn't already.

"Don't bother. I see now he's got the wrong height and build to be Radcliff—not to mention the wrong voice." There was a pause. "On the other hand, this one's voice is familiar. He might be some other deadbeat who owes me money. Go ahead and strike a match so we can see who it is, Lew."

Before Lew could commence fishing a match out of his shirt pocket, there was a sudden clatter of bottles heard coming from farther down the alleyway behind Hornet, followed by the sound of shifting feet. Looking over his shoulder, Hornet could just make out the vague outline of something or somebody detaching itself from a heap of crates, bottles and old burlap sacks of refuse. This was followed by a short grunt and the sound of running feet.

"Hey! There he goes!" cried Mrs. Brockbane, who pushed past Hornet in pursuit, followed closely on her heels by her two heavies. "Come back here, Radcliff!"

Left alone, Hornet exhaled with relief. Apparently, Radcliff, hiding there in the alleyway amid the trash all along, was abruptly thrown into a state of panic at the prospect of a struck match illuminating the alleyway and giving his position away. "That was as close a shave as I could desire," Hornet told himself.

Hornet was not out of danger yet, however. The commotion of a moment ago had attracted the attention of three or four drunken cowhands and revelers, who now began heading in the direction of the alleyway from the drag, as likely to aid someone in distress as to join in assaulting them, depending on who the victim was. "This way— the sounds came from in this alleyway," he heard someone say.

A second before they turned the corner into the alleyway, Hornet stepped aside. Concealed in a stretch of inky blackness along the wall, he went unnoticed by the group, who swept past him.

He listened a moment for any further sounds to indicate there were others coming, then skirted quietly along the wall until he reached the connecting back alley that led to the rear of Clancy's office. If he remembered right, his office was in the fifth building from this end.

He moved cautiously up the passageway, groping for any obstacle that might be in his way. Here, as in the side alleyway, the moonlight from above had no presence in the lower reaches. Once he stubbed his toe against a rain barrel that was just below the reach of his outstretched hands. About halfway down the alley, he stopped at what he believed was the rear door to Clancy's building. The ground floor contained a reception desk at the front, while the back rooms were used for storage. Above this were the offices, with the largest belonging to Tull Clancy himself.

Hornet tried the door. As he expected, it was locked. He gave it a hard kick with the sole of his boot and immediately wished he hadn't. The unyielding resistance and the pain that shot from his foot up his leg told him that an iron bar supported the door on the other side. Gritting his teeth against the pain, Hornet sat down and removed his boot to massage his foot.

After five minutes of this, he slipped his boot back on and stood up again. Ignoring the door, he instead turned his attention to the solitary window covered by a steel mesh. Moving his fingers along the uneven intersections of metal wires, he came upon a gap that was wider than elsewhere. Working the end of his gun barrel in the gap, he managed to entrap the barrel between the wires and then, pushing the gun up at the handle, snap one of the brittle wires. After breaking most of the rest, he then had free access to the window pane beyond it.

Now, with only the glass in the way, Hornet undid his neckerchief and wrapped the barrel of his gun in several layers so as to muffle the sound of shattering glass to come. As a precaution, he timed his hit to coincide with the next flurry of shooting and shouting from the town's main drag. He didn't have long to wait. In a matter of seconds he had broken through the thin pane and cleared away the rest of the jagged shards of glass so that he could crawl through the opening without injuring himself.

The frame was small, so it promised to be a tight fit for him, and all the more difficult with the bottom-most part of the frame at neck-level. Thinking of the rain barrel he'd bumped into earlier, he retraced his steps to it. A dip of his hand revealed that the water level came up almost to the brim. Gently upending the barrel, he poured out the contents, which immediately flooded the passageway, sending the water back down the alley to the larger alleyway he'd come through. If anyone at that moment should happen to be heading up the larger alleyway, their curiosity might well be aroused by the sudden flow of water, but, for the moment, that couldn't be helped, and he had an urgent use for the barrel.

Rolling the barrel up to the window, he stood it up so he could stand on the bottom end. No sooner had he applied his full weight to the bottom, however, than the wood panel gave way and he went crashing through the barrel to the wet but hard-packed earth of the alley. "Damnation!" snarled Hornet.

The staves and hoops seemed to be more sound than the rotted bottom, so he was still able to find a use for the barrel by tipping it over and standing upon its side. It was tricky work maintaining his balance on it, but by holding on to the window frame with his hands, he was able to keep himself upright. When he was ready, he hoisted himself through the opening, stopping about halfway in. From there, he wiggled his way further forward. It was when he shifted the position of his palm along the left frame that he felt a sharp stabbing pain as a shard of glass penetrated his lamb-skin glove. Again he cursed. Not pausing to examine his injury now, he continued to thrust himself forward. Landing on his feet would have been far preferable, but the confining space of the window frame meant he would have to land on his hands and trust that there was nothing sharp or otherwise dangerous awaiting him on the floor.

It was a crate filled with cans that broke his fall, sending him tumbling head over heels until he ended up on the wood planking of the floor. His first thought was to cock his ear and listen for the sounds of outside noises. Hearing none, he busied himself in wrapping his wounded hand in his neckerchief.

Looking up, Hornet saw a thin, faint strip of light outlining the door of the storeroom he was in. Quietly crossing the room, he reached the door. Finding it unlocked, he pulled it aside and entered a short passageway that led to the reception room. Here the light filtering in through the windows from the nearest street lamp might make him visible to someone passing by in the street outside, so he proceeded with the utmost caution, crossing to the staircase only when he was certain there was no sign or sound of anyone just beyond the windows. He mounted the staircase and eased his way up the steps. They creaked with each step, but there was no one to hear it. When he'd reached the top of the staircase, he looked up the darkened hallway. It was too dark to see the doors, but he guessed there were probably as many as four doors leading to four separate rooms.

Having never been inside this building, Hornet could only guess which of the doors led to Clancy's private office. He tried the first door and entered. Moonlight streaming in through a back window showed that it was a lesser room than Tull Clancy might be expected to occupy. The desk along the far wall was on the small side, such as perhaps a clerk or assistant might use. Nonetheless, he thought it might be worth his while to see if anything useful could be found in the room.

The moonlight was insufficient to read by, so he risked striking a match against the edge of the desk and lighting the lamp he found on the desktop. He turned the flame up only enough to cast a bare minimum of radiance needed to read by. He brought the lamp over to the first filing cabinet, upon which he laid it. He then began to wade through the many files. Not finding anything of interest after some minutes and growing bored, he skipped to the *H's* in hopes of finding something under the name of Hornet, but there was nothing there. He next turned his attention to the desk, which, after several minutes of searching, yielded nothing of value.

It was time to take a look at what might be in Clancy's private office. He went back out into the corridor with the lamp. Three doors remained. One led to a room similar to the first, which he didn't waste any time on.

The next appeared to be a meeting room, with a long table and six high-backed chairs. A pot of cold coffee stood on a side table. He helped himself to a cup before moving on to the last room.

Finding this room locked, he set the lamp down on the floor and stood back. He then threw his weight against the door, which yielded. The sound of the lock breaking seemed horribly loud to him, so Hornet paused to listen but heard only the chirping of night crickets, then the voices of a pair of revelers passing by out front.

He was now in a sparsely furnished antechamber with a desk, chair, single cabinet and leather couch along the wall. In all likelihood, this chamber belonged to a secretary or receptionist. Next to the couch was yet another door, which he assumed must be Clancy's private office and inner sanctum. If anything of importance was to be found, it would be beyond this door, so he gave no further thought to investigating the desk or anything else in the antechamber. Once again the door, he found, was locked and, once again, he forced it open. Before proceeding into this final room, he took the precaution of leaning a chair against the outer door of the antechamber. Should anyone happen to come in, unlikely as it was, he would hear it. After this, Hornet entered Clancy's office and closed the door behind him.

Inside the office, a large roll-top desk immediately attracted his attention. Setting the lamp down on an adjoining side table, he tested the sliding cover. It was, unsurprisingly, locked.

Going back into the antechamber, he returned with a couple of metal letter openers and a heavy paperweight he'd noticed on the desk there. Again closing the door, he set to work pounding one of the letter openers into the tight gap between Clancy's desk top and the bottom edge of the tambour near where the lock was. Once the letter opener had been wedged halfway in, he added the second one over the first as a reinforcement. He now had a reasonably strong crowbar to use. He put down the paper weight and forced the blades up by their handles. An almighty creak sounded as the lock split apart.

"Eureka," whispered Hornet as he rolled up the cover and began to rummage through the various pigeon-holes and drawers—none of which ended up containing anything of interest, however.

He next turned his attention to the eight drawers set deep in the two heavy supports under the desk top. Just one of the drawers—the left uppermost one— was locked, so he focused on that first. It was the work of only a moment to pry open the drawer with the letter openers. In it he found various letters, telegrams, certificates and an agenda— nothing much of value on the face of it.

And yet it had been locked, which would seem to indicate that there was something in it that its owner wanted kept hidden from view and not easily accessed.

He pulled out the drawer and checked for a false bottom. Finding none, he put it aside on the ink blotter and examined the space where the drawer had slid out from. Reaching in with his hand, he felt along the back panel, which seemed surprisingly solid and thick. He was about to retract his hand, when he thought he detected a difference or inconsistency in the wood somewhere. He ran his fingers all along the wood, carefully searching and probing with his fingertips. There it was again— a consistent groove where none should be. But could it be just a chance pattern in the grain of the wood? Hornet brought the light down to the level of the empty drawer and peered into it.

There it was. He could clearly see a definite groove running horizontally and two more, joined to it at right angles, running straight up to the underside of the desk top. They were faint but nevertheless there and formed an unmistakable rectangle.

Sliding his fingers across or pressing against the rectangle had no effect on it. His fingers then strayed to the underside of the desk top. It was only a few short seconds before he made contact with a small circular indentation. Hornet pressed it. There was a click and then another, at the end of which the entire rectangle slid out.

Reaching into the space of the secret compartment, Hornet was able to come away with a small leather bag.

Excited at his discovery, he immediately placed it on the desk and undid the drawstring. Inside the bag were two separate documents. He unfolded both and flattened them on the table under the light. The first was an unsigned contract between Clancy and Hornet's father dated eight years earlier. At the bottom was the word "witnesses" followed by four lines. These too were blank. The other document contained what looked to be a topographical map replete with extensive marginal annotations. There was, for example, a snaking line that indicated a river running across a corner of the map and a marsh to the south, but neither were familiar to him.

Returning his attention to the first document, Hornet sat down at the desk to read.

Telford Clancy, of Triangle X, agrees with

Richard E. Hornet, of the Double Z ranch, to the following terms.

On the day of their children, William Clancy and Hattie Hornet, entering into matrimonial union, it is agreed that possession of the jointly owned Clancy-Hornet cache of gold, previously mined along the disputed property line of their respective land-holdings, is to be inherited by William Clancy and Hattie Hornet, to do with as they wish.

Until the date of this aforementioned marriage, strongly advised to take place within one month of the 21st birthday of Hattie Hornet, the cache will remain inaccessible to all parties. Prior to the signing of this contract, the gold will be buried at a location chosen by Father Pierre-Jean De Smet, who is well known to both families and trusted implicitly. In order to ensure that neither party has independent access to the burial spot, it is furthermore agreed that Telford Clancy will receive a map drawn by Father De Smet showing the general tract of land within the territory of Wyoming where the gold is buried, while Richard E. Hornet will receive a map showing the precise spot within that tract.

In this way neither party will be able to find his way to the burial site without the aid and approval of the other.

If no marriage takes place, the gold is to be evenly divided and said division uncontested.

Hornet cast his memory back. The name of Father De Smet was familiar to him, though he reckoned he must have died seven or eight years ago.

He looked again at the topographical map. The

map showing the general area was so large that, even if it were localized, it would be all but useless without the missing half to show the precise location within that area. He imagined that his father's version, if it still existed, might be sketched on transparent paper that could be laid over the general map and would contain an "X" to indicate the exact position of the buried gold.

Though he'd certainly known about the gold and perhaps even the maps, he'd never heard his father mention any specific details about this unorthodox arrangement that he and Clancy had agreed to back in the day. He wondered why it had been necessary and why they hadn't simply divided the treasure. Or, if they didn't want to divide it, why couldn't it just be held in trust at a bank? An answer presented itself to him almost immediately. It was because Clancy didn't really trust banks and his father didn't trust Clancy's connections to bankers. That seemed as likely a reason as any.

The lack of any signatures on the contract also puzzled him. In his estimation, it could only mean one of two things. Either they never finalized the contract they had drawn up, or else this version was simply a copy of the original signed version.

It was a pity that none of the witnesses were referred to by name, or else he might know whom to consult to ask further questions.

As he pondered the significance of what he'd stumbled upon, Hornet heard a noise coming from the antechamber or just beyond the antechamber. Hastily he extinguished the lamp and pocketed the map and contract.

Chapter Seven

Hornet drew his gun and listened. How the devil could anyone have found him? Did they know he was here? Had he been betrayed by the deputy? Unlikely, if he was any judge of men. Besides, he wouldn't have known where in town he was. It must have been the puddle created from the barrel. Someone must have come upon it and investigated. This would have led to the discovery of the busted window. Now all hell was about to break loose. With perhaps a dozen or more of Clancy's men in town, it put him in a precarious position.

He heard the distinct sound of the chair in the other room giving way and then the door being slammed open against the wall. This was followed by rough voices and feet stamping across the floor.

Beads of perspiration broke out upon Hornet's brow. When the last door to the inner office was thrown open, death would come with it. He had to get out of there, and the only way out was through the window. He flung open the sash just as the door was thrown aside. He crouched down in the corner away from the open window so as not to make too visible a target. A red flame flared and the crash of a gun sounded from the doorway. Hornet leveled his gun and fired off two slugs. Several figures, who had been on the verge of charging into the room, scattered behind the door posts.

His enemies driven back momentarily, Hornet seized the opportunity to climb out the window. He already had one leg out the window and was all set to hang by his fingertips from the outer sill before dropping to the alley below, when he heard the sound of feet rushing through the dark from farther down the alley, or perhaps from both ends.

He glanced all about. Then he saw it. There was a drainpipe leading to the roof within easy reach of the window. It was the only avenue of escape open to him.

He glanced back again at the doorway. Someone from just beyond the door post was stretching his hand and, without daring to show his head, fired a blind shot that whined just inches past Hornet's neck. Hornet fired off one last round through the doorway to give his enemies something to think about. He holstered his gun. Then, taking hold of the drainpipe, he began to pull himself up hand over hand.

"There he goes! Out the window!" shouted someone from the doorway just as a bullet went screaming past Hornet's hip in the open window. Almost at the same moment, there was another shot fired from somewhere down the alley, resulting in a chunk of wood to Hornet's right side splintering. After scrambling up the last part of the drainpipe, he rolled onto the rooftop. There he lay on his back looking up at the faint outline of the moon, gasping for breath and grateful to be alive.

His enemies, however, did not stop to rest. Quite a bit sooner than he would have imagined, he heard the scraping of feet moving up along the drainpipe. A gun muzzle appeared over the roofline. Hornet, his eyes grown large, hastened to roll aside on the tiles as a spray of bullets sought him out.

If Hornet had a gift, any at all, it was the ability to think quickly and decisively in a moment of dire emergency. So it was that he immediately mimicked a cry of agony under the pretense of having been shot. Taking the bait, the gunman's triumphant, grinning face peered over the roof's edge. Hornet, ready for him, brought the barrel of his gun heavily down on the gunny's head. The triumphant face changed to one of shock and pain, then went blank as it disappeared from view. A moment later, Hornet heard the thud of a heavy body landing on the ground below.

A confused chorus of angry raised voices and curses broke out. Someone in the window called down to those below in the alley to circle to the side ends and front of the building in an effort to cut off Hornet's retreat.

Hornet was already on his feet and moving across the rooftop that rose in a gentle pitch, his gun back in its holster. He anticipated that it would be at least a couple of minutes before other gunmen would work up their nerve to venture out onto the roof from the window. It was two minutes that he intended to put to good use. Reaching the front of the building, he peered round the wooden parapet overlooking the street. There he saw men moving quickly to take up positions across the street behind posts and water troughs. There were perhaps three or four there, and at least a similar number at the back of the building.

Hornet's one great hope lay in the chance that no one had yet reached the side alley at the nearest end of the building. Speed was of the essence now, as it was just a matter of time before a rifleman or two would make their way to the rooftops of the buildings across the street, whereupon he would be an easy target. With this thought and the image in his mind of someone coming up the back way after him again, Hornet resolved to make a dash for the end of the rooftop to the right.

Reaching the end, he poked his head over the roofline for a moment and only a moment, only to draw two shots from below.

Hornet cursed. They'd gotten there sooner than he'd expected. He drew back, flattening himself against the tiles. From there, he dragged himself forward on his belly by the elbows until reaching the curved side of an eyelid dormer that marked the centermost point of Clancy's office building. There he lay amid pebbles and a rusted old tin can, for the moment undecided about his next course of action. His prospects seemed bleak, with his enemies apparently now after his life rather than being content with just capturing him.

It was also possible that his identity was not yet known. They might think he was nothing more than a common thief who'd broken into Clancy's office.

As if reading his mind and determined to dash his hopes, a harsh voice split the air. "Johnny Hornet. We know it's you up there. You're surrounded on all sides and haven't a chance of escape. Throw down your weapon and proceed back down the way you came up. Do this, and we pledge to hold our fire. We'll then be lenient with you— as lenient as you deserve. You've got one minute to think it over and give your reply. After that, you can consider yourself living on borrowed time and will, by and by, be blown off that rooftop."

The words that stood out most to Hornet were the words "as lenient as you deserve," which, it seemed to him, could be wide open to interpretation.

"Fetch the marshal, and I'll talk to him."

"Who in the hell do you think you're talking to now? This *is* Marshal Briscot."

"Were you among those as were shooting at me from the doorway to Clancy's office without any formal warning just now?"

"Never mind about that now. Are you going to turn yourself in or no?"

This settled matters as far as Hornet was concerned. The marshal did not even try to deny that he was among the group that had tried to gun him down without warning. He now knew that the only sort of mercy he could expect from the likes of Marshal Briscot was to be found at the end of a rope, especially if the man he'd struck over the head moments ago was dead. Perhaps he was foolish to have even in passing entertained the notion that the marshal was not fully in the pocket of Clancy.

Hornet stretched his neck to peer beyond the dormer at the way he'd come. There was no sign yet of anyone else attempting to get up onto the roof that way. Even as he thought this, he detected the vague outline of a hat, and as yet no face to accompany it, slowly rising. He sent a shot just wide along the roof edge to discourage whoever it was. Turning back, he sat up on his haunches. He felt reasonably safe for the moment with his back against the curve of the eyelid dormer. After having shifted his position, his hand chanced to come upon the can he'd noticed earlier. This gave him an idea. Re-holstering his gun, he set the can up on its end. He could feel in the darkness the still-attached lid bent down into the can. He drew out his pocket knife -- a useful tool somehow missed by his enemies when they captured him earlier. By inserting the blade of his knife down into the gap and twisting it back up, he was able to retract the lid. He then gathered all the pebbles about him and filled the can with them. When it could hold no more, he pressed the lid back down, then secured it with a length of rawhide wrapped twice along the can from end to end.

Hefting it in his hand, he took stock of its approximate weight and judged how far he could throw it with a degree of accuracy. It was heavy— perhaps too heavy to throw it with anything more than general accuracy. But that was all he needed.

Hornet stood up and turned his head for a last look over his shoulder to be sure no one was coming at him from behind. Taking several deep breaths, he readied himself for what lay ahead. In the dim light he could just make out where the line of the flat roof across the alleyway was. The space between the two rooftops was just shy of ten feet. Even with a running start it would not be an easy leap across. He might not fall to his death if he didn't reach the other roof, but he would almost certainly break a bone or two, and then be at the mercy of the gunmen waiting in the alleyway below.

Of immediate concern was getting across without being sighted and gunned down. To do that, he intended to distract their attention by throwing the can into the alleyway just before his leap across.

He almost immediately dismissed the idea of

throwing the can after he'd started his run. To do so might throw off his balance and lead to his falling short of the opposite rooftop. No, the only thing to do was to pitch the can first and then start his run immediately after that.

Putting aside any further doubts before they threatened to unnerve him, Hornet drew back his arm with the can gripped firmly in his hand and aimed for the general area of where he thought the bottles were that he'd seen earlier. He threw it. There was an almighty initial crash, followed by secondary sounds as the can bowled over other objects in its way. In response, he heard surprised curses and gunfire, which informed him that the can had landed in about the best spot that could have been hoped for.

On the heels of the throw, while the gunmen remained in a state of confusion, Hornet sprinted toward them and launched himself over the gaping void. The seconds that it consumed were like an eternity. As soon as his feet left the roof, he knew that he either wouldn't make it or else it would be by a whisker. Only at this moment did he realize that he had underestimated how far he could jump. As he passed over the chasm, he saw fleeting images of enraged faces, illuminated by the flash of gunfire as the gunmen now began to direct their fire upwards at the figure streaking over them.

With just inches to spare, Hornet's right foot followed by his left alighted on the edge of the opposite roof. Had he fallen just short and struck the roof hands-first and hung there, he'd likely have received a spray of bullets in the back before he could swing himself up and over the roofline to safety.

Having found purchase on the roof, his

momentum propelled him forward. Directly ahead in the dark loomed a chimney stack that he seemed destined to speed past before he could slow. He never got that far, however, because it was at this same instant that a gunman came out from behind the chimney stack and stepped into his path.

Chapter Eight

The gunman's eyes grew big as he saw the fast-moving figure hurtling toward him. Before Hornet, with a full head of steam, could begin to pull up, he ran heavily into the gunman, knocking him over like a bowling pin. Spinning apart, they fell sprawling a dozen feet from each other. The gunman had received the worst of the collision and was slower to recover. After a quick shake of the head to rid himself of the stars dancing before his eyes, Hornet picked himself up off the rooftop and started toward the gunhand. Desperate circumstances spurred him to seize the initiative. It was essential to overcome the gunhand quickly before anyone else could come to his aid. The man, looking groggy after the collision, was just getting to his knees when Hornet reached him. With one hand he took hold of the man's bandana to steady his target and with the other drove his fist against his mouth. The head snapped back, and he seemed half finished already. But before Hornet could land a second punch, the gunman got an arm up to protect his face, with the result that Hornet slammed his fist into the bone of the man's forearm close to the elbow, which hurt like the devil. Hornet staggered back, nursing his wounded knuckles with his other hand.

This gave the gunman, still on his knees, the opportunity to go for his revolver. Although Hornet couldn't see it, he knew from the gunman's movements outlined against the night sky what he was up to. Hornet gave a swift kick to where he judged the gun would be coming up. There was a howl of pain and the clatter of a fallen gun. Hornet followed up the kick with a merciless barrage of blows to the man's face and midriff.

He kept up his assault until the gunman had stopped struggling and was unconscious. Hornet found the gunman's fallen gun and slipped it into his belt. Having an extra gun couldn't hurt. It would also be one less weapon his enemies could use against him.

Hornet got up slowly. There was a twinge in his back and his knuckles throbbed with pain. His one thought, even during the fight, had been to reach the far end of the rooftop so he could drop down into the next alleyway, but already he could hear the voices of men moving along the back alley to cut him off. The fight with the gunman hadn't lasted much more than a minute, but it had been long enough for the other gunmen to cut off his intended escape.

To remain on the roof, where he was now known to be, was to court death. Running through his train of thought was the sudden appearance of the gunman. Where had he come from? How did he get onto the roof here? Hornet checked the vicinity of where he had

72

first sighted him. It took only seconds to find what he was looking for: a trapdoor set in the roof just beyond the chimney stack behind where the gunman first made his appearance. In all likelihood the man, reacting to the sounds of a commotion, had just come up through the opening and stepped out from behind the stack.

Hornet drew back the door on its hinges and peered down into the darkness. In the dim light he saw the first few rungs of a ladder. He had a vague recollection of the building being used as a storehouse and also being owned by Clancy. All was quiet below. He doubted if his enemies were even in the building yet. If he could hide down in the storehouse somewhere, he might be able to slip away later on.

But first things first. Sparing a moment to eject the spent cartridges of his gun, Hornet jammed fresh rounds into the empty chambers.

Opening the trapdoor, he descended the ladder. The trapdoor operated on springs, so it fell back into place behind him, shutting out all light. His nerves were on edge as he made his way downward in the dark and into the unknown. It reminded him of the time he was a child and was exploring an old abandoned mine. At the end of one of its shafts was a long ladder that led to a lower chamber dug out of the earth. On a dare, he descended the mine ladder, which seemed like an endless descent into a nether world populated by bats, winged demons and other creatures of the eternal darkness.

As he thought of this, he realized that he had come to the end of the ladder and was now somewhere on the floor of a storeroom. He paused to listen but could hear no sounds from within the building. His eyes roved to where the room's closed door, edged faintly with light, was. The door led, he supposed, to one of the front rooms of the storehouse that faced the street, which no doubt accounted for the light source.

Hornet struck a match and scanned the room, which, he saw, contained piles of crates, baskets and earthenware jars. As he stepped toward the door, a creak sounded from the floorboard under his feet, and on the heels of this another creak was heard, this time from the nearby door. *Someone was opening the door.*

Chapter Nine

Hornet blew out the flame and drew his gun. Standing stock still, he waited as the door continued to open. When it was about halfway open, it stopped. Though he strained his ears, he could hear nothing in the deathly silence, apart from his own heartbeat and an occasional street noise from outside. He tried to control his breathing, inhaling and exhaling slowly and evenly so as to make as little noise as possible.

Eventually he moved toward the door at an angle. As he did so, the same floorboard from before creaked again. Biting his lip, he tightened his grip on his gun, the muzzle of which was directed at the gap between the door and the door jamb. Then, as the creaking of the floorboard began to abate, the door swung slowly shut.

Relief washed over Hornet. He was now all but certain that it had been his stepping on the warped floorboard that originally triggered the opening of the door. Screwing up his courage, he stole quickly across the dust-covered floor toward the door. In this part of the room there were no stacked boxes or anything else in the way, so he was able to reach the door without stumbling over or into anything. When he finally reached the door, he had a look at what lay beyond. It was a rectangular hall that connected to a front room through a door that was ajar. There were two more doors at either end of the hall and three at the back, one of which he was now in. In addition, there were two ladders at each end of the hall leading to upper-storey rooms.

He was debating what next to do, when, from the front room beyond the hall came the sound of men entering the building. Accompanying them was a flood of yellow light that poured into the hall through the door that stood ajar. Someone, he perceived, was carrying a lantern.

Hornet backed up into the storeroom and closed the door just a moment ahead of the door across the hall being opened. His door had creaked as he closed it, but it was drowned out by the simultaneous noise of the other door being opened.

Hornet stood rooted to the floor facing the door inside the storeroom, undecided for the moment what to do. The sounds of two voices, mere feet away, reached his ears as clear as a bell.

"Which way is the room leading up to the roof?"

"Straight ahead through that door there."

Hornet gasped. There was no time to move out of sight. The nearest crate to hide behind was twelve paces behind him. The timing of their arrival couldn't have been worse.

About to be discovered, he did the only thing he could. Squaring his shoulders, he raised his gun toward the door, ready to deal death to whoever was about to come through it.

He heard the sound of the door knob being turned, then the sound of the door turning open on its creaking hinges— but still the door did not move toward him, for it was not his door but the neighboring door that had been opened.

"No, not that door. It's the next one down the hall."

By the grace of God or sheer dumb luck, Hornet had been granted a reprieve. He now had just enough time to rush to the wall adjacent to the door and flatten himself against it. The door flew open. He caught the doorknob in his hand, preventing it from rebounding and possibly drawing interest in what the obstruction was behind the open door.

Three men filed into the room with guns in their hands. The first also carried a lantern, which he swung left and right as he looked about.

"Smitty must still be on the roof."

"Shh. Keep your voice down," cautioned the oldest of them. "Let's not tip him off to our presence— assuming he doesn't already know we're down here. And turn down that lantern, you fool. There's the opening up ahead already.

The light was extinguished and the lantern, no longer needed, was set on the floor. Only a timid stretch of light came in through the open doorway behind them, but it was enough to see by.

The three figures, casting long shadows, proceeded to the foot of the ladder, where they made their way cautiously up the ladder one at a time. The leader paused just before the trapdoor and looked back down at the others, little more than vague outlines in the dark.

"Al," whispered the leader to the gunman just below him on the ladder, "you sure Smitty said he might go up this way to the rooftop?"

"That's what he said he had a notion to do, but who knows? If he did go up there, I'm thinking we'd have heard gun play or some other commotion by now."

The leader gently lifted the trapdoor a couple of inches with the muzzle of his gun and peered across the roof for an initial look, limited as it was. He then closed it again so he could consult with the others. They were faced with something of a dilemma. If they tried calling out to Smitty, who may or may not be on the roof, they risked exposing their position to the man they hunted. The apprehension and tension of the moment brought out the worst in the three, who began to quarrel in angry whispers punctuated by curses, every word of which carried to Hornet's ears behind the door.

Knowing that they were there to kill him, Hornet felt no sympathy for their state of agitation and even enjoyed a sense of satisfaction that he was in no immediate danger.

The leader, a coward at heart, still hesitated to go up through the trapdoor. "The wisest course of action may be to just wait here and catch him if he tries to come down this way."

The other two scoffed at this suggestion. "Our orders were to get up on the roof," said one of them, "and deal with him if he's still there. Even now he might be slipping down some dark unguarded part of the building or crossing to the next building. If we're up there, we'll be in the best position to alert the others or else fire on him."

"I agree with Al," said the third gunman.

"All right. Shut up, the both of you," replied the

leader, who now felt compelled for the sake of his reputation to go up. "Keep alert and keep close behind me." Having given his instructions, he put aside his reservations and summoned up the necessary courage to venture out onto the roof. Raising the trapdoor again, he slipped deftly and almost noiselessly onto the roof. Once on the roof, he rolled away from the opening with his gun extended so as to make a less inviting target if he should be sighted. Spotting the chimney stack, he scrambled toward it and flattened his back against the bricks with his gun hammer cocked. The other two, close on his heels, followed suit.

Before the last gunman was halfway through the trapdoor, Hornet came out of his hiding place and slipped through the door, closing it behind him. It would not take the three gunmen long to discover their unconscious confederate and to deduce that he, Hornet, may have come down through the trapdoor earlier, but he surmised that he had the advantage of at least a five-minute head start on them. It should take perhaps that length of time or longer for them to confirm that he was no longer anywhere on the roof.

Hornet crossed the hall and entered the front room of the storehouse. The accumulated dirt of many years dimmed the windows, making it difficult to clearly make out objects in the street outside. But this disadvantage was also an advantage, as it ensured it was unlikely that anyone outside would see him as anything more than a vague shadowy outline.

Chancing a discreet look out the nearest window, he saw that there were at least two men openly brandishing rifles on the boardwalk across the street. Their heads were tilted up toward the roof, which is where they thought it most likely that he would appear.

Keeping low, Hornet crept back the way he'd come, into the hall again, out of reach of the probing rays of the street lamps. He tried several of the hall doors. None of the rooms he looked into offered a good place to hide. One door led to nothing more than a closet. Eventually he found a large back storeroom that, like the room with the ladder and trapdoor, was piled high with boxes, crates and barrels, all in neat rows.

At the back of the storeroom he found a single grimy window high up in the ceiling, which he concluded was the eyelid dormer he'd sheltered against when up on the roof. There was also a back door, which he could use later to escape from the building if the opportunity presented itself. Hornet, about to turn back to the rows and head down one of them in search of a crate to hide in, suddenly noticed something that he'd almost overlooked at first glance. There was a large corner wardrobe standing against the wall next to the door, far apart from the rows of crates and things. Its twin doors stood open, and inside, behind a single long topcoat that hung on a hanger, was just enough darkness to shield him from view.

It was such an obvious place to hide —so visible, right in plain sight— that it might just be overlooked.

It was also about the worst place to be if he were discovered, however. There would be nowhere safe to flee to, be nothing to duck behind as there would be if he were holed up somewhere in the rows of crates, barrels and boxes. It would be nothing for them to drill him.

Any last doubts were dispelled when he heard the sounds of approaching footsteps in the hall. Hornet quickly ducked into the wardrobe and crouched down behind the topcoat. To lessen the chance of drawing attention to the wardrobe, he left the twin doors open.

Voices came to his ears now. He guessed that there were at least three men.

"Ed, Charlie, fan out. We're to search this room from top to bottom."

A minute later, the alley door flew open, and two more gunmen came in. One of the men already in the room happened to be in sight of the door. Startled, he drew his gun, then lowered it when he recognized who it was.

"Damnation, but you gave me a fright. You boys oughten to barge in like that. I was on the verge of opening up on you."

One of the newly arrived gun toadies guffawed in response.

"Shut up, Rawlings," said a voice that Hornet recognized as belonging to Jake Malloy, who was the other newcomer. "This is serious business, and I won't tolerate any horsing around till we find him."

The offender muttered a surly excuse. The two other gunmen came up now, and Malloy addressed all three. "What about the other rooms? You boys check them yet?"

"Crosby and some of the others are going through them now. We were told to check this room."

"And the roof?"

"Shady, Al and Hugh went up there; and what do you suppose they found?"

"Just tell me; don't make me guess like I'm some snot-nosed kid of yours in need of teachin'."

"They found Smitty stretched out on the roof, just coming to. He'd been battered good. His head was all but bashed in."

Malloy swore. "No sign of Hornet anywhere then?"

"None at all."

"What was Smitty doing up there ahead of the rest?"

"He'd gone up on his own initiative. Only told Al he would."

"Damn fool. Will he be all right?"

"Al and Hugh are helping him to Doc Severin's now. Said they'd rejoin us when they got back from there."

"And Shady?"

"Left him on the roof to guard the trapdoor in case Hornet was to go back up."

"Good thinking. So, appears he's either slipped out of the building, which ain't so likely, or he remains within the building somewhere. It's up to us now to give it a good going-over. How far you three get in this room?"

"We just this minute come in."

"All right. You three go through the first rows from the far wall and we'll start from this side. We keep at it till we meet in the middle. And I want a thorough as possible search, Leave nothing unturned."

After about ten minutes, the two groups of searchers had checked everything apart from the two centermost rows.

Hornet felt relieved that thus far nobody had thought of checking the wardrobe.

His thoughts were interrupted by the alley door opening again.

Malloy turned toward it. "You," he said to the newcomer. "What are you doing here?"

"I've come to lend a hand in the search."

"Well, we're almost done in here, but if you want

to chip in, you can help us search through the last two middle rows."

"Sure," he said, closing the door behind him. The newcomer scanned the room filled with bored men overturning and kicking boxes and the like and looking inside anything that might be big enough to hold a man. His eyes fell on the wardrobe and lingered there. Hornet couldn't see the face but could see him clearly from about the waist down. As the seconds passed and he still stood there, Hornet grew increasingly anxious.

"Anyone think to look in here?" said the newcomer with a flick of his thumb in Hornet's direction.

"The wardrobe?" asked Jake, looking out from behind a stack of boxes. "He'd have to be a fool to be in there, almost in plain sight, but you're welcome to take a look."

"Think I will," said the newcomer, stepping toward the wardrobe.

Chapter Ten

His heart racing, Hornet tried to make himself as small as possible behind the coat for the little good that it would do him. Beads of perspiration stood out on his forehead as the man leaned down and brought his face forward.

Hornet reached for the gun in his holster, but what chance did he have against six gunmen in the room, and more outside? If he shot this man, which was easily enough done, he still faced insurmountable odds. He knew his limitations, and he knew that he might well be the worst shot with a handgun in the room. Like the Indians, he'd always felt more comfortable with a long gun, in or out of the saddle.

Then he saw the face of the man, and their eyes met. Incredibly, the man winked, and he knew why. He was staring into the face of none other than Deputy Marshal Tom Dugan.

The deputy, after making a show of carefully

checking the wardrobe's contents in case anyone was looking his way, withdrew and said, "Nope. As empty as a spent cartridge in here."

Minutes later the gunmen completed their exhaustive search of the room.

"What now?" asked one of them.

"Half of us'll move on to the next building and see if there's any sign of him there. The other half will scour the streets." As the men began filing out of the room, some out the back door and the rest out the front way, Jake Malloy stopped one of them. "Charlie, we'll need someone to stay behind here and guard this room from the inside. If Hornet's still somehow in this building somewhere, he might try to come here to hide, and I don't think any of us will want to have to search this room again."

Charlie, nodding, sat down on a crate and began to roll himself a cigarette.

Just as he was about to follow the others out the back door, Malloy spotted the deputy lingering near Charlie. "What about you, Deputy? Care to join us?"

"Nah. Think I'll stick around here for a while. I'd like to get up on the roof and see what there is to see. Maybe I can spot signs of where Hornet might have made his way down from it."

"Good thinking. You know the way up there? Go left out into the hallway and one door down. Inside that storeroom you'll see a tall ladder that leads to the roof. Here, take my lantern with you; you'll need it," he said, handing it to the deputy.

"Thanks, Jake."

Let me know if you find anything. I'll be seeing you."

As the foreman headed out the back door to join the other searchers, the deputy disappeared out the opposite door, headed, apparently, for the other storeroom.

Some minutes later, Hornet heard the deputy's voice again. "Come here a minute, Charlie," he said from the hall doorway. "I need you to help me with something."

"I really shouldn't be leaving the room."

"It'll just take a minute, Charlie."

Hornet heard the footsteps of Charlie departing the storeroom. Finally alone now, he wondered if this might be his opportunity to venture out of the wardrobe.

Before he could decide, he heard the returning footsteps of, he assumed, one of the two men. But which of the two was it? Whoever it was crossed the room and stopped in front of the wardrobe.

"We're alone now."

"Deputy Dugan?"

"That's right. I've just sent the guard on a fool's errand that'll occupy the next couple of minutes at least. If you want to get out of there and be free of your enemies, there's no better time than now."

Hornet got up and stepped out of the wardrobe. He stretched his arms as he stood facing the deputy. "I sure am obliged to you for this. To think, I actually was wondering earlier on if maybe you were the one responsible for setting those gunmen on my trail."

"A day ago, and I probably would have, but my perspective's different now and I'm conscious of being beholden to you for saving my life. Lucky for you, you didn't kill anyone today, or else I really might have had to take you in."

Hornet would have spoken, but the deputy,

cocking his ear, held up a restraining hand. "I think Charlie's already coming back. Come on— and pull your hat down so anyone seeing you with me in the dark will likely think you're one of them."

The deputy opened the back door and looked up and down the alley, then up along the rooflines. "We're in luck. Nobody's out here just now." He closed the door behind them.

Dugan and Hornet crossed the narrow passageway to the door of a boarded-up house directly across from the storehouse. The door was unlocked— in fact, had no functioning lock. "Come on. Quickly now." In they went, Dugan again shutting the door behind them.

"This house has stood abandoned for some time now. I know about it because I've had occasion to evict trespassers and vandals," said the deputy. "We're fortunate that none of Clancy's men are in here now searching the rooms. I can about guarantee they've been here more than once today."

They passed through several other rooms and a corridor on their way to the back end of the dilapidated house, which years before had been the pride and joy of some now-forgotten home owner. Once beyond the first room, the deputy lit a match. It wasn't long, however, before there was sufficient light coming through the chinks in the boards of the rear windows ahead, so the deputy put out his match.

"Whereabouts you leave your horse?" asked Dugan as he peered through a gap in the window. Outside was a neglected kitchen garden, overgrown with crabgrass and other weeds. At the far end was a toolshed and the fragments of a picket fence that marked the rear boundary of the property.

"It's to the east of town, near that crossroads where I last saw you."

"Guess you'll have to circle to it. If I were you, I'd make it a very wide circle. No telling if you might run into one of the searchers along the way."

"I'll try my best to avoid them."

"Here's where we part. I don't think you will, but if you've got any sense left in you, you'll get as far away from here as you can and never come back. Oh, and you'll also take that sister of yours with you."

"I've been through too much to just give up now. There's somebody killed my father and somebody behind a lot of other wrongdoing. I think you know who I mean."

"You can't change the world all by yourself."

"No, but I can try to change what's not right with Tull Clancy and his band of cut-throats."

"Son, Tull Clancy *is* the world here. The sooner you get that into your head the better. Go against him, and you go against insurmountable odds."

Without another word between them, they once again shook hands and parted company, Deputy Dugan back the way he had come and Hornet to the outskirts of town and eventually to his horse, if it was still there.

◆ ◆ ◆

The searchers couldn't keep watch over all the ground leading out of town. It took time, patience and keenly alert senses to avoid them, but within an hour

Hornet was at his horse. Untying the sorrel, he led it farther into the woods until he came to a glade where the light was better. There he stopped to unfold the sheaf of papers he'd stolen from Clancy's office. Soon realizing that the light from the wan moon, even in the open glade, was too feeble to read by, he lit a match and held the flame over the first sheet.

"Ain't a signature or name anywhere to be seen in this document," Hornet said to himself. "But that doesn't mean it can't anyway yield up a name." He furrowed his brow in concentration. "Unless I'm very much mistaken, I've seen this handwriting before, which I know to belong to Lawyer Lanaghan."

Hornet refolded the documents and put them away. Just then, his horse tipped his muzzle up at him and snorted, as if to ask, "Where to now?"

Hornet stroked his horse's neck and answered, "Ralph Lanaghan doesn't know it, but he's about to receive an unexpected visitor."

Chapter Eleven

The knocking went on until someone inside the mansion opened the shutters to an upstairs window and glowered down at the visitor. "Who's down there? What do you want at this time of night?"

Hornet, looking up, removed his hat. "I'm sorry to disturb you, ma'am."

"Not half so sorry as the people of this house that you woke up. We'd all just gone to bed within the hour. It must be nearly midnight." The woman, wearing a night bonnet, pulled her shawl tighter at the neck as if to stress how cold and also how inconvenienced she was. Extending her head further out the window, she peered down at the caller. "Who'd you say you were?"

"It's John Hornet. I've got to see Lawyer Lanaghan about a matter of urgency."

"I don't know you, except by name. I knew your father, but he's dead now," she added as if it weren't already known to him.

"If I could just see him for a few minutes, I'd by mighty grateful."

"This isn't the time to call on decent folks in their homes. If you've business with my husband, then come back in the morning. He'll decide then whether to receive you or not."

"As I said, it's awful urgent. It has to do with Tull Clancy."

She was about to close the shutters, when a sedate voice spoke to her from within the room. "It's all right, Martha. I'll see him now. Tell him to wait by the door, and I'll be down directly."

Hornet heard a short muffled objection expressed by the lawyer's wife and then a muffled retort before the invitation was passed along to him.

It was Lanaghan himself, holding a candelabra with a single candle burning, who opened the door to him a minute later. He was dressed in nightclothes and a nightcap. A sleepy-eyed house servant appeared just then from below stairs to ask if he could be of service, but Lanaghan waved him away. Then, changing his mind, he called the servant to his side as he beckoned Hornet into a room.

After a short exchange with the servant that Hornet did not hear, the lawyer joined Hornet in the room.

Hornet found himself in a panelled study lined with books on law, history, politics and philosophy. The thick, sooted ceiling beams were hung with landscape prints, wood engravings and framed newspaper clippings. The lawyer set the candelabra on the oak-beam mantel next to a richly decorated urn.

There was a knock on the door. It was the servant returning with firewood in his arms from the rack of an adjoining room. After filling the grate under the chimney with the wood, he lit a fire and left the room. "Good night, sir."

"Good night, James. See you in the morning."

With the room already beginning to warm, Lanaghan sat down in a plush chair behind a massive mahogany desk. At Lanaghan's invitation, Hornet sat down in a second chair at the other side of the desk across from the lawyer. Although Lanaghan had an office in town, it was apparent that he occasionally had visitors and clients calling on him here at his home over a mile outside of town.

"Now, then," began Lanaghan, studying his visitor. "Seems I know you from way back, Johnny, though it's been years since I laid eyes on you."

"That's right, Mr. Lanaghan."

"Your father and I used to have some dealings back in the day, though his regular lawyer was old Samuel Puttman. My condolences to you, by the way, on your loss."

"Thank you, sir."

"Dick Hornet was a good man."

"He was."

"I'm sure I could tell you quite a few inspiring stories of the old days involving your father."

A mood of sad reflection entered Hornet's mind at the mention of his father, prompting him to look down from the lawyer's eyes to the desk.

"Well, death is a part of life, unfortunately," added Lanaghan in a sympathetic tone. "They go hand in hand. And when you reach my age, you'll find it touches you much more often, with relations and old friends one by one departing to a better place."

Hornet suddenly felt ill at ease and conscious of having imposed on his host. "I'm sorry I disturbed you so late at night, Mr. Lanaghan. I didn't realize what hour it was before I came here. Now that I'm here before you, I feel like after all I maybe should have waited till morning."

"Don't worry, Johnny, now that I'm here and willing to listen to what you have to say. I assume you wouldn't have come out here if it hadn't been important." The lawyer lifted his bushy eyebrows, which under the firelight highlighted the rows of wrinkles spanning his forehead. Hornet interpreted it as a sort of prompting for him to say what he was there for. It was as though Lanaghan was determined not to appear too eager to initiate a discussion involving Tull Clancy.

"I guess I better come to the point as to why I'm here," began Hornet, lifting his gaze from the table. He firmed up his jaw and sat up straighter, a renewed sense of purpose taking hold of him. His eyes, bold and earnest again, met Lanaghan's. "I'd like to know about any business dealings between Mr. Clancy and my father that were conducted with your help."

Lanaghan looked puzzled. "Why, none at all, as far as I can recall."

"Maybe I should be more specific. I'm speaking about a contract you drew up for them."

It was almost imperceptible, but Hornet noticed a slight stiffening of the lawyer's back. "Contract? What sort of contract is it you're referring to?"

Hornet reached into his pocket for the contract and spread it before Lanaghan on the desk. "This one here."

The lawyer put his reading glasses on and studied the document. His face, losing some of its color, seemed to register recognition at sight of the document. After a moment, he looked up at Hornet. "Where did you get this from?"

"I'll talk about that some other time. For now, I was wondering if you could tell me what this all means."

"What makes you think I would know anything about this?"

"Isn't it in your handwriting?"

Lanaghan's head went down again. "Why, so it is," he confessed.

"Then would you please tell me more about it."

"Tell? There isn't much *to* tell. There isn't much to this at all." He laughed dismissively. "It's not of any great consequence."

"I'm no lawyer, but that's not my impression."

The lawyer laughed again, though Hornet thought it forced. "Is it signed? Has it been certified? No." Frowning, he shook his head. "This is nothing more than a draft related to an agreement that never came to anything. Therefore it has no legal value."

"I'm not so sure that it never came to anything. I seem to recollect my father speaking to me about a wedding gift of immense value that my sister was to receive."

"Your father was a fanciful man full of fanciful notions at times. He sometimes spoke about something before it was a sure thing, as it appears he did in this case. He shouldn't have done that."

"My impression is there's something to it."

"Well, your impression is wrong, Johnny."

"Then what happened to the gold from that mine? I've never seen it or heard about it except in connection with my sister's wedding."

Lanaghan spread open his hands and shrugged his shoulders. "Sorry. I can't help you there. I've no idea what became of the gold. I can only assume that Mr. Clancy and your father finally decided to split it. What they did with it after that is anybody's guess."

Not liking this answer, the younger man frowned.

"Of course," continued Lanaghan, "it's entirely possible that your father overestimated the worth of that gold. The market value might only be a small fraction of what he originally thought it would be. Maybe your father ended up exchanging his share of the gold for, say, a hundred head of cattle or less."

Hornet's frown deepened. "A hundred head of cattle, you say? Then there'd be a record of that."

"That's just one example," the lawyer hastened to add. "There are lots of ways to dispose of raw gold. Some men gamble it away in a single night sitting at a card table, maybe in no more time than it takes to down a couple of drinks."

"So you say."

"I'm just trying to help you by offering logical alternatives to something nefarious, which, unless I'm very much mistaken, is the way your thoughts are running at the moment."

Hornet, who was beginning to distrust Lanaghan the more he spoke, didn't answer this. His thoughts were already moving ahead to a new point. "Well, seems to me there's an easy way to find out if there was anything to that contract. You can just let me know who those four witnesses were, and I'll check with them about how matters stand."

"I'd like to help you, Johnny, but there's such a thing as client-attorney confidentiality. That's something I've always held sacred."

"That's for clients. These four aren't clients; they're just witnesses."

To this, the attorney had no immediate answer. He yawned as if to indicate that their interview was almost over. "Well, hmm, yes, but I've always held the identity of witnesses in the strictest confidence as well."

"Have you now?"

Lanaghan now went on the offensive. "Maybe it's time you told me where you got this draft from." As if to reinforce what he said, a wall clock chimed the hour.

"Let's just say I found it somewhere."

It was the lawyer's turn to frown. "I know for a fact that it rightly belongs to Mr. Clancy. You'll understand that as his attorney, I feel it my duty to take possession of it and return it to him." Lanaghan began to slide it toward himself.

Before the paper had reached the edge of the desk on the lawyer's side, Hornet put the flat of his hand on the paper, halting its progress. "Mr. Clancy can have it back when I'm through with it, but not before then," said Hornet in a tone that was just short of menacing.

The lawyer's eyes narrowed a moment as he nodded. "As you like, Johnny. I'm not going to force you to give it up; but you understand that this will have to be reported to Mr. Clancy. I don't think he'll like hearing that you're going around with a document that belongs to him."

"You tell him I welcome a visit from him so we can sort all this out between us."

Lanaghan, leaning back, removed his glasses and tapped his fingernails thoughtfully on the desk. "Where shall I tell him he can find you?"

"Well, I would have been at my family's ranch, but, as you know, somebody burned it down a while ago. Maybe I'll just come to him one of these days."

There was a hint of a smile playing on the thin lips of the lawyer. "I'm sure he'd like that."

"As a matter of fact, I was already out his way earlier today."

"That so?"

"Yeah. But I never got to see him. I only got to speak with his son William and his foreman, among others. Nice fellers, by the way. They have a way of making you feel at home."

Ignoring the younger man's conspicuous sarcasm, Lanaghan carried on. "I'm sorry you missed your chance to talk over the document with Mr. Clancy when you were out there."

"I didn't have it then. It was later on I found it."

There was a lengthy interval of silence, too long to be anything but ominous in Hornet's opinion. It was finally broken by an outburst of chuckling coming from the lawyer. "I've heard it said more than once that you have a reputation for being headstrong, Johnny."

"William Clancy used a similar term when speaking to me earlier today."

"Did he now? Well, he was right." Still smiling and with his glasses back on the bridge of his nose, the lawyer picked up the sheaf of papers and made a show of studying it again. "Let me see now... I might be able to help you after all. I don't off hand remember who those witnesses were, it being so long ago, but if I read all the way through the contract, I think it'll help to jog my memory."

Hornet sat back and allowed the lawyer to read and think in peace.

Lanaghan, clicking his tongue in annoyance, glanced over his shoulder at the firelight and back again. "The light's too weak here. I'll take it over to where there's more light." Pushing back his chair, Lanaghan brought the sheaf with him to the fireplace. There, bending over the sheaf with his back to Hornet, he pretended to read. A sinister smile played on his lips in the glow of the firelight as he deliberately dropped it into the fire.

But before the sheaf could reach the hungry flames, its descent was arrested by Hornet's hand reaching past the lawyer. "Good thing I was standing right behind you when you dropped this valuable document," said Hornet.

The lawyer, taken by surprise, turned his head. "I didn't hear you leave your chair."

"I've got a soft tread."

"Yes, it was a good thing you were there to prevent it from falling into the fire," said the lawyer through clenched teeth as he turned the other way and circled back to his desk. "I can't think how I could have been so careless."

"Neither can I," replied Hornet in an ironic tone.

As they settled into their seats again, Hornet folded the papers and slipped them into his pocket. Now more than ever mistrusting Lanaghan, he was on the alert for sudden signs of movement from him. Even as he gave the impression he was solely focusing his attention on the papers he was tucking away, his eye was able to detect the movement of the lawyer's right arm, which was opening a drawer.

Hornet lunged across the desk, and was just in time to block the long-barreled gun that Lanaghan had been in the process of raising. A squeeze of the wrist bones prompted the lawyer to drop his weapon.

The younger man picked up the gun and retook his seat. "What were you aiming to do with this?" he said, pointing it at the lawyer.

Lanaghan, scowling, rubbed his wrist. He looked as though he wouldn't say another word. Then, with a crafty smile, he said, "I wasn't going to kill you, Johnny, if that's what you're thinking— not unless you had forced me to."

"That's comforting."

"I was going to hold you here until the Clancys could come for you. I suppose you know that I know you've caused them a great deal of trouble."

"They've been here to see you then? You've spoken to them today?"

The lawyer nodded. "That's right. They were here earlier whilst hunting for you. I don't think they thought there was much chance of you coming out this way, and neither did I, or else they'd have left one of their men behind to receive you."

"They know I have this contract and map?"

Lanaghan hesitated, as if debating whether it was wise to answer this question. He finally shrugged his shoulders. "They'll know it now, when I tell them. Seems that no one who was in the office after you knew it was missing. Only Mr. Clancy himself would know that next time he was in there. His men could see you'd been interrupted while ransacking the desk."

"How'd they know I was there?"

"You left a trail a blind man could follow. All that water in the alley was bound to be discovered sooner or later, and then it was easy enough for someone curious to notice the window had been broken into. The marshal figured it might be you when word got to him that someone had broken into Mr. Clancy's office, and this was then confirmed when several men caught a glimpse of you as you went out the window."

"Well, that's just as I thought."

"I know all about your busy day today, Johnny. There are men— dangerous men, killers— on the look-out for you, and they won't stop till they find you. You can save yourself some trouble by turning yourself in. That way you might live."

"Your threats annoy me, old man."

"There's nothing you can do about it."

"Can't I? We'll see about that. First of all, before I leave here, you're going to give me that list of names on the document. I want to know who all four of them are."

"Give yourself up, you and that sister of yours. Your time is limited as it is."

"Now you've really got me riled up. You can only push a man so far. I'll be damned if you haven't put me in a killing mood." Hornet lifted the gun and pressed its muzzle against the lawyer's forehead. "I want those four names, right now."

Beads of perspiration stood out on Lanaghan's forehead. "You can't scare me. I've never been the scaring type."

"I'm not trying to scare you," snarled Hornet. "Are you going to give me those names?"

"You wouldn't! You aren't the type to kill in cold blood, Johnny."

Hornet exhaled and lowered the gun. "Guess you're right. I'd be lowering myself to the level of the Clancys."

The lawyer wiped the perspiration from his forehead with his sleeve and breathed more easily.

"Guess I'm about through with you," said Hornet, standing up. "It's time I let you get back to your sleep."

"Hold on a minute," said Lanaghan. "There are some things I'd like to discuss with you first."

Hornet was about to retake his seat, when he grew suspicious. "You suddenly seem anxious for me to remain here. I wonder why..." Hornet looked at the door. "Where's that servant of yours?"

"What do you mean? He's in bed of course."

"Is he? No chance you sent him to fetch the nearest Clancy gunmen?"

Before Lanaghan could answer, Hornet strode across the room and threw open the window, letting in the cold night air. His ear cocked and one eye watching his host, he listened.

He heard it. Not far off. It was the beating hoofs of a dozen horses being ridden hell for leather.

"I might have known!" exclaimed Hornet as he sprinted for the door, pausing only long enough to throw it open, then doing likewise with the outside door. Once clear of the house, he raced to his sorrel, which he'd left on a hillside copse overlooking the lawyer's mansion.

Just as he reached his horse, the first of the horsemen, rounding a turn in the trail, came into view.

For a moment, as the horsemen swept by the foot of the steep hill, Hornet thought he could slip away unseen. One of the gunmen, however, happened to turn his head to scan the surrounding terrain. Although

Hornet was amongst the trees, his outline must have stood out against the night sky.

He heard a raised voice giving away his position. The mass of gunmen, pulling rein, skidded to a stop, turned and unleashed a fusillade of lead in Hornet's direction. Bullets tore through the thicket, scattering chunks of bark. But Hornet was already on the move, threading his way through the trees and down the slope in the other direction. A slug whined just past his ear as his head disappeared behind the far side of the hill. An open stretch of ground now lay before him that led to the dark edge of the forest.

The horsemen raced for the low point of a gully that skirted the west side of the hill.

Hornet, however, was on a fresh mount and made for the densest part of the forest, thick with aspen and spruce trees. By the time he was again in view, he was entering the forest and disappearing into the shadows.

"Well, horse," muttered Hornet, "we may not have learned any of the witnesses' names from that lawyer and almost got shot up in the attempt, but it's just occurred to me what one of those names might be."

Chapter Twelve

Having eluded his pursuers, Hornet paused by a dense growth of black-hawthorn trees half a dozen miles from the lawyer's house. He'd been following a westward stream he knew would eventually lead him to the home of Nathan Nettle, who'd formerly been a close friend to both his father and to Clancy. Although he had been unable to learn the names of the four witnesses from the lawyer, he guessed that one of the four might just be Nettle. It seemed, to his mind, a logical assumption.

But the closer he came to his destination, which wasn't far from the Graysons' homestead, the more his mind became troubled with thoughts of what had become of his sister. Was she still there or somewhere in the surrounding woods? Or had she already been taken to the valley?

He felt he had to know, so he swung his horse from the bank of the stream and headed for the Graysons' homestead, which was only a few extra miles out of his way.

As he drew within sight of the farmhouse, he saw no lights on or signs of any life. This was not surprising, as the Graysons would likely already be in bed at this hour. Leaving his horse at a grove of trees, he cut across a pasture that was to the left of the farmhouse and the windowless side there. Along the way dozing cows, their scent strong in the air, lifted their heads to look in his direction. Some studied him intently. Others were completely indifferent.

Reaching a stand of trees that gave him a view of the front of the house, he paused to look and listen.

He was close enough now, he thought, to have attracted the attention of the dogs. That was his first clue that something was not right. The second clue was what he saw in the open window of one of the upper-storey bedrooms. Although darkness reigned across the face of the window, there was a distinct pinpoint of light just above the window sill. Every few seconds it stirred, floating outward from the window, almost like a firefly, and then back again. It had to be a cigarette. Someone was sitting in the window looking out. There was something else he noticed. At first he thought it might be just a shadow of a tree branch across the whitewashed sill and whitewashed clapboards of the house. Looking more closely, he felt confident that it was the barrel of a rifle.

It could of course be Bill Grayson keeping watch for fear that the Clancys might raid the farmhouse again in order to capture Hattie. This, however, was unlikely, as Grayson would have his dogs to rely on. No, all things considered, it was much more likely that this was one of Clancy's men left behind to draw a quiet bead on him,

Hornet, should he think of returning.

He quickly angled back the way he had come, eager to fall back to the house's blind spot where he could not be seen from any of the front windows. Upon reflection, he thought it likely that there was also a gunman stationed at a window at the rear of the house.

To all appearances, the Graysons had abandoned their farmhouse. But what of the cows all about him and the rows of crops that required tending? Would they have just left everything with no one to look after the livestock and crops? Unlikely, unless the Graysons had been driven away and prevented from returning. Knowing Bill Grayson, he wouldn't have stood for that. He'd have enlisted what support he could from neighbors and friends and made an attempt to retake his holding.

As he headed back, Hornet noticed one of the cows, more curious and less shy than the rest, rise up from where it had been resting and begin to follow him. Unfortunately, it had a cow bell around its neck, and with each step it took the bell clanged. Fearful that it would attract the attention of one of the gunmen, Hornet stopped cold in his tracks. The cow, also coming to a halt behind him, stood still to stare dumbly at him. Not content to only stare, it stretched its neck and sniffed him. Hornet turned to face it and let out a low growl, prompting it to retreat a few steps. This added to the clanging, but not much. For the moment it kept its distance and was content to continue staring at him.

Relieved that the cow had stopped making noise, Hornet was beginning to think of being on his way again, when he heard a door creak open — signifying, to him, that one of the gunmen was venturing out to investigate the noises he'd heard.

If he remained where he was, Hornet was sure to be sighted. Nearby was a stone feed trough, in front of which was a cluster of dozing cows. Making quickly for the trough, he brushed past them and dropped down behind its length into the dirt to lay still. Unfortunately, his sudden movement toward the trough had disturbed the cows, most of which had risen and moved off. This brought more clanging to the ears of the sentries.

Catching his breath, Hornet listened and heard the light movement of feet and the jangle of spurs. Someone was just on the other side of the fence that marked the boundary between the side yard and the start of the pasture. Slowly and without noise, Hornet eased his gun out of its holster and held it ready.

"You see anything, Ben?"

Hornet could hear the other gunman spit out his chewing tobacco before answering. "Could've just been some cows moving about for whatever reason."

"They don't usually stir like that without cause."

"Suppose you're right. Let's take a closer look at what's out there."

The dreaded sounds of gun hammers being pulled back and the bodies of the two gunman climbing over the fence and dropping down onto the earth came to Hornet's ears.

As soon as they'd hit the earth, a commotion broke out. A wild pig that had been hiding in a straggle of bushes a little farther along the fence, came charging out, having been frightened by the gunmen. One of the men, in turn startled, swung his six-gun toward the sounds and fired a wild shot.

"A boar! That explains why the cows were spooked," said one of them, putting away his gun.

"Nothing for us to do out here. Let's get back to the house."

Hornet's luck had held. So far it seemed that that was all that had separated him from an early death. With the gunmen gone, he picked himself up off the ground and brushed off some of the dirt from his trousers. This wasn't the time to linger for long, however,

He was about to turn to leave, when a thought occurred to him. He had a vague recollection of a shack set apart from the farmhouse about a half-mile distant. He remembered that in the old days it had been inhabited by one of the Graysons' farmhands. Returning to his horse, Hornet swung into the saddle and made his way to the shack, giving the farmhouse and surrounding pastures a wide berth.

When he arrived at the shack, it, like the farmhouse, showed no initial signs of life. Perhaps it hadn't been inhabited for years. The farmhand, whose name he couldn't remember, might, for all he knew, have died years ago.

Tethering his horse to a nearby sapling, he approached the weather-worn shack with caution. Its solitary door stood open. Constructed out of mud bricks and logs, there was a single window at the front and back ends. Entering the sagging hovel, he looked about. There were only two rooms, both sparsely furnished. The first served as the living room and, to the side, a kitchen with an old range and a small crooked table. The back room was the bedroom. It was difficult to tell if the shack was still inhabited or if it hadn't been used for ten years.

Suddenly a voice spoke from out of the darkness somewhere behind him. "This old shack ain't much to look at, is it?"

Hornet, taken by surprise, whirled, his hand instinctively going to his gun. In the doorway was a tall, broad-shouldered figure.

"I didn't know anyone lived here," said Hornet, relieved to see that it was the farmhand.

"I don't get many visitors."

"Didn't you hear those shots up by the farmhouse just now?"

The hand nodded.

"And you didn't think to investigate?"

"House and surroundings ain't safe no more— not with them intruders there. Not at night."

"No. I can attest to that."

"They're lying in wait for someone. They want to gun him down."

"That would be me," chuckled Hornet.

"You?" said the hand with a puzzled look. He seemed to be struggling to connect the noise he had heard with Hornet's presence here.

"That's right. I suppose they let you stick around to tend the livestock and see to the crops."

"You suppose right." There was a pause. "So you're the one."

"Yeah."

"It's a danger even to talk to you."

"They tell you that?"

He nodded.

"They tell you anything else?"

"Yeah."

"Well? What?"

"That I'm to turn you in if you show."

Hornet preferred to pursue another avenue of conversation. "You know where the Graysons went?"

Another shake of the head. "They didn't tell me. Said would be better for me not to know."

"That sounds sensible. Anyway, I think I know where it was."

"Had a brother. Saw him cut down in the prime of life afore my eyes. We was charging the Yanks up a hillside at Manassas. Was the third volley come down that took him. He was just ahead of me— one rank away. I seen him fall. He was my brother— my little brother I'd known all my days. I stopped to cradle him. He was goin' fast. His blood was runnin' on me—over me. He said, 'Don't leave me— don't leave me, Gus. I don't want to die alone.' I said, 'Hush now,' like to a child; 'I won't never leave you.' I held him tight as though it could bring new life to him when the old one was fast running out. 'Tell the folks I send my love! Tell 'em I didn't shirk my duty and was brave when my time come. Tell 'em!' I swore again I would. 'I'm fading fast, Gus,' he said, his voice weakening so's I had to put my ear to his mouth. 'This is it. This is what it's like to die.' Speaking seemed to exhaust him, and a shiver run through his body.

"Then the captain come to say, 'Son, you got to let him go; we need every man jack of us to drive the enemy off this hilltop. It's a hard life, but we have to leave the consoling for later.' I turned and looked up, tears full in my eyes and clouding my vision, at the captain's face. I said, 'Don't you worry, Cap'n. He's gone now. I'll be along.' And so I laid my brother's head down softly 'pon the grass. He had a almost peaceful look on his face, near to smiling. Then I picked up my rifle where I lay it and continued my charge up that hill."

"The war— that war— was a lot of years ago," said Hornet, hoping to get his mind away from it and back to the present.

The hand continued as if Hornet hadn't spoken. "We carried the fight to 'em that day, we did, by gawd. A thousand of us crying out the rebel yell as we threw ourselves against them like waves against a rocky shore. We lost a lot of good boys, including my brother, but we won that hill. They got the worst of it and turned tail when they seen there was no quit in us."

"I'm sorry, Gus, but I'm in a hurry. You notice if my sister went with the Graysons?"

The hand blinked a half-dozen times as if to clear his vision. "The Graysons?" repeated Gus. "They left this morning. Loaded up their wagon. Said they didn't know when they'd be back. They said I ought to come with them, but I didn't want to. I don't know any other place but this. I don't want to go to anywhere that I don't know. There might be people there who don't want me. It's better here."

"Did you notice if they took my sister with them?"

"Sister? You got a sister?"

"That's right. She's got blonde hair and is a few years younger than me. She was wearing a blue gingham dress last I saw her."

"There was such a girl riding in back of the wagon with the Graysons. She was pretty, but not for the likes of me. Was that your sister?"

"I think it was. I appreciate your telling me, Gus. I reckon they took her to a place of safety."

"I had a brother once. Saw him cut down afore my eyes..." began the farmhand again.

Hornet listened for a while to a repeat of the man's story. Twice he tried interrupting him to tell him he had to leave, but the hand, in his other world, continued to recount the past.

Hornet eventually slipped quietly away. Gus had his back turned to him and was looking out the back window. He could still hear him speaking in the still air as he mounted and rode away.

Chapter Thirteen

It was a relief for Hornet to know that his sister was, if Gus' account could be trusted, out of danger for the time being. This freed up his thoughts to work on clearing up the unsolved mystery related to the map and the missing gold. Hopefully, speaking to his father's old friend, Nathan Nettle, might go some way toward putting the missing puzzle pieces together.

After returning to the stream and following it for a couple miles, Hornet left it again, heading south-west by south, before finally arriving at Nathan Nettle's holding. Once prosperous, he'd suffered a series of misfortunes, culminating in the sudden stampede of two hundred of his best steers that perished after falling into a ravine. At the time, it was strongly suspected that the Clancys had been behind it.

Hornet had already made up his mind to wait till morning if there were no lights burning in the main house of Nettle's ranch. To his surprise, there were several windows that were illuminated. After looping his reins about the hitch-rack out front, he strode up to the door.

He was about to knock, when the door was opened wide by Nettle's daughter, Simona.

"Johnny Hornet! I looked out the window just now when I heard someone ride up. I could hardly believe it was you."

Hornet removed his hat and spoke slowly, perhaps uncomfortably. "I'm real glad to see you again, Simona."

"I told myself I wouldn't cry if I ever saw you again," she said, turning her head slightly away as she fought with her emotions.

Hornet started to grip her arm but resisted the impulse, suddenly conscious of feeling he hadn't the right to. He thought of how striking she looked in the light, with her delicate, well-formed lips and silken hair cascading down her shoulders. Though not beautiful by the standards of most men, she possessed an inner loveliness and quiet dignity that he'd always admired in her.

Simona looked back at him, her eyes now beginning to well up. "Your face is bruised and your clothes caked with earth."

"I'm all right."

"When did you get back?"

"Less than a week ago. I came as soon as I'd heard about my father's death. Then, upon arriving, I suffered a second blow when I learned my sister was missing."

"Life's been terrible to you and your family of late,

Johnny."

Hornet shrugged his shoulder.

"You never did say goodbye before you left."

"Wasn't time."

"I was told you left because you'd done something wrong."

"No. Whoever said that is a liar. I was driven out. Someone took a shot at me on the trail near our spread— missed me by a cat's whisker. I could have stayed, but Dad counseled me to leave and come back when things had cooled down."

She smiled wistfully. "Just so you know— I didn't really believe what I'd heard. Not in my heart of hearts. I told myself a long time ago that I'd only ever believe it if I heard it directly from you. In the meantime, what anyone else said was just noise to me."

"I appreciate your faith in me, Simona."

"Johnny, I want you to know that both my dad and I were at your father's burial service. He was a great man. You must miss him terribly."

"I'll be all right. I'm over it now."

"I hate when you do that."

"Do what?"

"Trap your emotions inside and act like nothing can harm you."

"That's not how I am— not really."

"Isn't it?"

Hornet shuffled his foot, resentful at being put on the defensive and even more resentful at not being able to find better words to express himself.

"You told me you loved me in the week before you left. Do you remember?"

"I remember."

114

"And that's all you have to say on the subject at this time?"

"Simona..."

"So the words come hard to you now, do they?"

"It's not easy for me—"

"For you to say again what you said once before?"

"Let me finish. I was about to say it's not easy for me to talk to you— not always. In the past, it always seemed like I had to work my way up to it."

"You're not going to start that again, are you? About how you feel unworthy of me?"

"I can't help how I feel and how my nature is."

"Yes, you can. Of course you can— if you want something — or somebody— bad enough."

"Things are worse than they were. I had something before, whereas now I hardly have a penny to my name. That fire at our ranch that took my father also took everything I might have one day owned. I had to sell off the last of our stock the other day just to settle the debts. Even still, there are some that remain outstanding."

"Since when did a man need money to tell a girl he loves her?" Distraught, Simona tossed back her mass of auburn hair and turned to walk away.

Again he hesitated, but this time he followed her and seized her from behind by the upper arms, which forced her to halt. As he swung her back toward himself, he could feel that she was shivering— but whether it was from emotion, revulsion or even cold, he could not say.

Her head looked down a moment, then up into his eyes. With a long sigh of relief, she threw her arms about him and sobbed as she buried her head in his shoulder.

"You care about me, then?"

"Of course I do. I couldn't not care about you if I

tried."

"Oh, Johnny! It's so good to be with you again. I don't mind telling you I was sick with worry all this time you were away."

"I can take care of myself," he replied, his pride reasserting itself.

In his ear came a whispered recrimination about another matter. "You didn't write to me, Johnny. In the eight months you were away you didn't write once. It bothered me that you didn't."

"But I did. Maybe you didn't get my letter?"

Simona searched her memory. "You don't mean that short letter to my parents?"

"It was to your folks, yes, but also to you."

Too elated at being reunited to quarrel, she instead laughed.

Their lips sought and found each other. Her lips were as tender and yielding as he remembered them. "Mine was always a love that was so strong it hurt," she avowed. "It seems like heartache is all I ever got out of it. But now, with you here again, I can forget that heartache for the moment."

Before Hornet could answer, they heard the sound of approaching footsteps, prompting them to disengage their arms.

"Simona? Are you there?" said her father's gravelly voice as the door to the far end of the entrance hall opened. "I thought I heard voices." Then, when Nathan Nettle caught sight of Hornet, he added, "I'll be damned."

"How-do, Mr. Nettle."

"To see you is almost to see a ghost, my boy."

"You look about the same, sir."

Nettle eyed him as though with suspicion.

"Though I wish I could, I can't quite say the same about you. You look as though you've been through a briar-patch. Guess Simona didn't notice that, did you, Simona? No, you were too starry-eyed or something. Shut the door behind you and come into the parlor for a sit-down, Johnny."

"Pa..." began Simona.

"Go and fetch some iodine and dressing, Daughter. That's what he needs the most from you at the moment. And I reckon Johnny'll be hungry as well. See if you can't serve him some of that leftover venison we had this evening. Don't worry. You'll be able to talk to him some more soon enough."

"You can see my father thinks very highly of my skills as a house servant," said Simona, who glanced back with a wry smile as she left the hall.

"I heard you were back in town, Johnny," began Nettle when he and Hornet had seated themselves in the parlor. "Ordinarily I'd probably ask you how you feel about being back, but seeing those bruises makes me think that not all is well with you."

"Frankly, being back has brought me nothing but trouble."

"Oh? What sort of trouble?"

"Let's just say that I've run into some unsavory people who don't wish me well."

"Well, you know you can always count on being welcomed here."

"Thank you for saying so, Mr. Nettle."

"Oh, and my deepest condolences on the loss of your father. There are few men finer than he was, living or dead."

"Thank you for saying that too. I'm touched by

your sentiments. And maybe I shouldn't go around saying this without any direct proof to offer anyone, but my gut feeling is that the Clancys were behind his death."

Nettle surprised him by the candidness of his reply, which was just above a whisper: "I always thought so too, son."

Simona returned carrying a small basket of medicines, dressings and ointments. After seeing to Hornet's wounds, she left again for the kitchen.

"That's a fine girl, my daughter," remarked Nettle, "if I do say so myself."

"I know it."

"She'll make someone a wife to be proud of someday."

"I don't doubt it."

"Forgive my frankness, Johnny. I didn't mean to prod you in a certain direction. I believe in letting nature take its course. But maybe you should know that she thinks an awful lot of you."

"And I hope you'll forgive me when I say that I didn't come here for what you thought."

"Oh? You're not here to court Simona, then?"

Hornet shook his head. "Maybe if these were happier times, but they're not. No, to say the truth, I didn't even think she would be here. Last I heard, she was off at college somewhere in the East."

"She just got back for the term break." Nettle, taking out his pipe, filled it with tobacco and applied a match to it. "Does Simona know you didn't come here for her?"

"I never got the chance to say anything. She seemed so... so overjoyed to see me. And now I don't know if I have the heart to tell her that I came here to see you and not her."

"She's an understanding girl. I'm sure she won't take offense— or not much. But my advice, if you don't mind me giving it, is to play straight with her and at some point let her know how you feel about her, one way or the other. I don't think it's any secret that she still carries a torch for you, John."

"Your advice is sound, sir."

"Now then: what was it that really brought you out here?"

Simona, returning, came in with a plate of cold venison, bread and a slice of cherry pie. She set it down in front of Hornet on a low table.

"I didn't realize I was so hungry," said Hornet, beginning to devour the contents of his plate. "Thank you, Simona."

"Coffee as well?" she asked with a smile of contentment. "I've got some from earlier this evening that only needs warming up."

Hornet nodded enthusiastically.

She returned a few moments later with a steaming cup.

"Thank you," he said, smiling up at her despite his mouth being full.

Simona would have stayed and joined them, but her father asked that they be left alone for some minutes while they discussed a "matter of some importance."

"Where were we?" said Nettle.

"I was about to tell you what I was here for."

"Oh, yes."

"Mr. Nettle, have you any knowledge of a certain contract drawn up between Mr. Clancy and my father?"

Nettle's brow drew together in contemplation.

"Why, yes; yes, I do."

"And were you one of four witnesses who signed under it?"

"You're right again; but how did you know about that? Your father tell you?"

"It was just a guess on my part; I thought it likely, seeing as how you were close to him, and to Mr. Clancy at one time, I believe. What I'd like is to learn everything you know about the agreement that was signed."

"Your father never told you about it?"

"Well, only in passing. He never went much into detail about it. In fact, the details were so scant that I never really put much stock in it or took it seriously."

"I think he probably wanted to keep it as close to a wedding surprise as possible."

"Well, there won't be any wedding now."

"Well, this is news to me. I'm sorry to hear it's been called off."

"Then you haven't heard yet what happened to my sister?"

"No, I haven't. Would you like to tell me about it?"

Hornet shifted in his seat as he became uncomfortable about the subject. "Let's leave this subject for another time, if you don't mind."

"As you say, son. Getting back to the contract, there isn't a lot I can tell you. As I understand it, it was a compromise reached with the best interests of both families in mind. Your father and Mr. Clancy couldn't agree on who should get the lion's share of the gold they'd dug up. Each felt he had a right to more than the other. If you ask me, however, I would say that your father was the one who had the stronger case."

"Knowing Clancy's character, I suspect you're

right."

"Oh, but he wasn't nearly so bad in those days. But as the years passed, he became greedier and meaner with money."

"Which sounds about the opposite of my dad."

Hornet asked several more questions, but Nettle wasn't able to give him much more information than he already knew.

When they'd finished conversing, Simona returned and chatted amiably for the next half hour. When she and Nettle sensed that Hornet was getting too weary to talk, the daughter and father carried on speaking to each other, paying no regard to the late hour.

Hornet leaned back, feeling comfortable and at home. He was struck by how at peace he felt here, far away from his enemies. He had begun to feel drowsy after the meal and the ordeals of the day. If he'd been alone, he might have fallen asleep right there in the chair.

As he sat back with his eyes half-closed, a sound from somewhere in the house, perhaps in the kitchen, came to his ears. "I can hear you two aren't the only ones awake at this late hour," commented Hornet.

"That must be Barkley," said Nettle.

"Barkley? Is that one of your ranch hands?"

"He's a ranch hand, yes, but not one of ours."

Upon hearing this, Hornet, who was only a moment ago on the verge of dozing, opened his eyes fully. "What ranch did you say he was from?"

"He's from one of the far-away ranches to the east. I don't recall the name now."

Hornet sat bolt upright, all thought of weariness banished for the moment. "If he came from that way, he would have passed through or near Clancy territory."

"What are you saying? You think he's one of Clancy's men?"

"I don't know. He's a stranger to you, right?"

"Never laid eyes on him before. He came in earlier today just as the boys were heading into town, this being pay day. He's on his way to some point shy of the Platte. He said his horse was a little lame and could he rest up here a few days before moving on. I told him he was welcome to bed down in the bunkhouse and that he could have free use of the larder back of the house. I reckon that's where he is now."

"I don't like the way he looks at me," remarked Simona.

Her father stared back. "You didn't tell me that."

She shrugged her shoulders. "I didn't think it was too important, and, besides, he's not staying long."

"Anyone else in the house?" asked Hornet.

"Just Billy in one of the back rooms who does the cooking and young Joshua, the chore boy."

"I don't wish to alarm either of you, but I have reason to believe he's one of Tull Clancy's hired guns and is here to put me out of commission."

"Oh, Johnny!" exclaimed Simona.

"What?" said Nettle. "What makes you think he'd want to kill you?"

"It's already happened once tonight that a couple of his gunmen were lying in wait for me over at the Grayson's farmstead. Luckily I was able to get away without them seeing me."

Nettle and his daughter exchanged looks of concern. Nettle was the first to speak. "Is this anything to do with that gold cache you were talking about?"

"Yes. That and a few other things."

"What gold cache?" asked Simona.

"It was gold that was meant to be shared between Hattie and William after they were married, but the Clancys are determined to get all of it," he explained to her. "Your father can explain it in more detail to you later." Then, to both of them, he added, "It's me that this Barkley wants. I don't think he's any danger to anyone else here. Just the same, I'd keep an eye on him if I were you and maybe think about having one or two of your men from the bunkhouse who's handy with a gun come and stay in the house while he remains here. That is, when they get back from from cutting loose in town."

"We'll be sure and do just that," said Nettle.

The three sat in silence as the sounds from the larder dwindled and the back door swung shut, suggesting that the stranger was no longer in the house. As a precaution, Hornet made his way to the larder, looking everywhere that the gunman might be concealed. He then locked the door and retraced his way back to his hosts.

"Well, the sooner I depart, the safer you two'll be. I thought of asking to spend the night here, but I don't think it's wise of me to stick around under the circumstances."

"I wish you'd stay nonetheless, Johnny," said Simona. "I'd feel safer knowing you're here."

"You'll be safe enough, Simona," he replied. Just keep the doors locked and sleep with a gun handy— the both of you. I've locked the back door. Be sure to lock the front door behind me when I leave."

"It's a pity you won't get a good night's sleep here after all."

"I'm just glad I found out about Clancy's man being

here. I can get my sleep elsewhere."

Hornet put on his hat and readied himself to depart.

"Where are you headed?" asked Nettle.

"I don't exactly know. Maybe if I could speak to someone else that has knowledge of that contract, it might help."

"What about Lawyer Lanaghan? He's the one who drew it up."

"I've already been out to see him. I got a very warm welcome, I can tell you, and very little information from him for my trouble. As a matter of fact, he tried setting some of Clancy's gunmen after me."

"What about Charlie Sykes? Do you know him?"

"Should I? Hmm, the name's a little familiar."

"Well, he was one of the other three witnesses to sign it. I happen to know, because he signed it at the same time I did. As for the other two who came after me, I've no idea who they might be."

"You didn't all sign it together at once?"

"No. Maybe that's how it's usually done, but not in this case. Two signed together, then the other two later on. And, as I understood it, your father and Mr. Clancy each signed it twice in the presence of each pair of witnesses."

"Fine. I'll start with Charlie Sykes then. Do you know where I can find him?"

"Yes. Head east along the east-west stream for a couple miles, then turn off just before the bend. From there it's a little tricky."

"Oh, Dad, I can show him," interjected Simona. "I know the way."

Both her father and Hornet were adamant that

Simona stay with her father.

After receiving the remainder of the directions, Hornet said goodbye and thanked them for their hospitality. Simona prepared a packet of food for him.

"You'll come again soon?" asked Simona as she lingered alone with Hornet just inside the door.

"I'll come when I can, Simona," he said, pulling her close and again finding her lips.

Once outside, Hornet unhitched his horse and led it away on foot so as not to alert the gunman to his presence. When he judged he was out of earshot, he swung into his saddle and sped away.

Minutes later he heard the sound of someone riding hurriedly after him. It could only be the gunman, he surmised, despite the precautions he'd taken. Pulling off to the side of the trail and retreating into brush, he drew his gun and waited.

Amid the sound of beating hoofs, a figure rounded the turn in the trail and came into view in the moonlight.

Hornet pulled back the hammer of his gun and steadied it; then he lowered it. Etched against the moonlit sky was an unmistakably feminine outline.

"Simona!"

The girl, seeing him, pulled up. He came out of the brush into full view. "What in the world are you doing on my trail, Simona? I might have shot you. It never occurred to me it could be anybody but the gunman."

"I'm coming with you, Johnny!" she exclaimed.

"What? Haven't we already been over this? There are men out looking for me. I wouldn't dream of putting you in that sort of danger."

"That's all the more reason why I have to come with you. Don't you see that it would drive me out of my mind sitting at home waiting hours and days not knowing if you're dead or alive? Now that you're back in my life, I don't intend to lose you, Mr. Johnny Hornet. Besides, you can use me as a guide to Mr. Syke's house. You've never been there, so if I show you the way, you'll save time."

"Look— it's impossible, Simona. Alone, I might have a chance, but two of us will make twice the target. So just turn around and go back home— please."

"Aren't you forgetting something?"

"What's that?"

"Unless you're prepared to use force, there's nothing you can do to stop me. Whether you like it or not, I'm not going to leave you."

Hornet growled in frustration.

"Look, I'll promise you this. I'll ride along with you only as far as Charlie Sykes' cabin and no farther. After that I'll either head back home or stay for a day or two at my friend Carol Renworth's house that's only a few miles from where Mr. Sykes lives and there await news from you."

"Does your father know you went after me?"

"Yes. He also tried to prevent me but was unsuccessful."

"I had a feeling you'd say something like that."

"So you'll let me come along?"

"Come on, then, Simona," he said, turning his mount back onto the trail and flicking his reins against its shoulder. Simona, tapping her heel against her piebald's ribs, joined Hornet at his side.

Chapter Fourteen

They could see the glow of the dying fire bathing the surrounding hillsides long before they reached their destination. Reaching what had been the cabin of Charlie Sykes, they began to sift through the wreckage. The hope was that Sykes had been away when the fire broke out, or perhaps that he'd gotten out of his cabin in time and was now elsewhere.

"Mr. Sykes built this cabin just a couple of years ago with his son," remarked Simona as she helped to pull away a charred board. "It was small, but he was like a proud father over it."

The cabin was in a clearing near a bubbling spring. Having found an old bucket, they made several trips there and back to put out the last of the fire.

"Didn't he used to live in town somewhere? What

was he doing out here?"

"He considered this his retirement home. He wanted to get away from people. More than once he said he preferred the company of animals. He was originally a zoologist by training, so this was a good place for him to study wildlife. He also cared for any animals that he found injured and would nurse them back to health."

Behind the ruined cabin were the remnants of a lean-to, inside of which were a half-dozen shrivelled bodies of what had been representatives of various species of woodland creatures. Some were in makeshift cages made of metal wire.

"Poor things," said Simona as they continued their search.

When they finally found Charlie Sykes' remains amid the debris of the cabin, they pulled him aside and folded his arms across his chest.

"I can only hope he went quietly in his sleep from the smoke long before the flames reached him," said Simona.

"I wonder about that."

"What do you mean?"

"Is Sykes' death just a coincidence? Or could it possibly have something to do with the Clancys?"

"I don't see how it could."

"Don't you?" Hornet knelt down alongside the body to examine it.

"What are you doing? Oh, Johnny— don't. Don't touch him. What do you expect to find?"

Two minutes later he answered her. "This," he muttered. After having turned the blackened body over, he'd traced his fingers along the back until he'd found three well-defined holes. "It wasn't the flames or the smoke that killed him. It was somebody shooting him in the back."

Simona's fist went to her open mouth. Horrified, she turned away from the sight. Hornet turned the body over again, then covered the face with an old saddle blanket that had escaped the flames.

"Why would anyone want to harm him?" asked Simona over her shoulder. "It doesn't make sense."

Hornet didn't answer. He was turning things over in his mind. It was too much of a coincidence that Sykes had been gunned down not long after he'd freed Hattie and was being pursued by Clancy's henchmen.

Simona spoke again, still with her back turned. "You spoke earlier about your confrontation with the lawyer and how you asked for the names of the witnesses. And we know that Clancy's gunmen are after you." She turned abruptly toward him. "Oh, Johnny, what if, for whatever reason, they've decided to kill all the witnesses. What if— what if that man we left with my father wasn't just there to kill you if you showed up? Oh, God. What if he was also there to… to..."

She never finished her sentence.

"Simona, let's get back there! We may still be in time!"

◆ ◆ ◆

Guilt, anxiety and fear of being too late conspired to make it feel to Hornet as though he was riding at a snail's pace rather than as fast as his fatigued horse would carry him. Simona's horse had staying power and hadn't been out all day like Hornet's horse, so she had no trouble keeping up

He had debated momentarily whether to, as before, leave his mount at a distance from the ranch and then proceed cautiously and stealthily toward the house on foot. He decided instead to ride straight up to the door, making as much noise as possible to alert everyone there of his arrival. The sounds of someone arriving, he reasoned, would thwart any attempt on Nettle's life that the gunman might be in the act of carrying out. Unfortunately it would also result in the disadvantage of attracting the attention of the gunman, who would almost certainly come out to investigate who it was who was coming.

"Simona," he reminded her over his shoulder for the second time, "whatever you do, stay well back when I ride into the yard. I'll signal to you as soon as it's safe."

Simona was about to answer, when the heavy discharge of a long gun was heard coming from the direction of her ranch.

"Oh, God! We're too late!" she cried.

"Keep back, keep back!" Hornet warned her as he drew nearer. There on the ground just in front of the house lay a body, its dark form revealed under the glow of a lamp in one of the windows. Behind the body stood the open door.

Heedless now of the danger to himself, Hornet didn't slacken his pace and raced up to the figure. He skidded to a stop and sprang from his horse, gun in hand. Even as he began to turn over the body of what he was sure must be Nettle, he glanced about for any signs of his assassin. Hornet couldn't have been in any greater of a disadvantage where he was, just under the light, whereas everywhere and everything else around him was cast in deepest shadow.

Having turned the body over, Hornet gazed into the face. *It wasn't Nettle.* It was the face of a man he'd never seen before.

Simona, having seen the prone figure from a distance, uttered a cry and rode up to join Hornet despite her earlier promise to keep back till all was clear.

"Thank God!" she cried. "It's the gunman. But where's my father?"

There was a nearby sound, and from around the left corner of the house a figure came into view.

"Pa!"

Simona ran to him and threw her arms about him. Hornet put his gun away.

"Take it easy, my girl. I'm all right," said Nettle, gently detaching her arms. "Did you think I wouldn't be?"

"Yes— well, I didn't know what to think. I naturally assumed the worst when we came upon the body out here."

Nettle walked to the body of the slain gunman, where he found Hornet crouching over it. "You look as though you could do with a refreshment, young man. Come inside."

Hornet stood up. "I guess we shouldn't have worried about you."

"No, you shouldn't have."

"What happened?"

"Knowing what he really was, I kept my eyes and ears open. I put out the lights and thought I would sit off to the side of the open window for another hour or so before turning in. The lights being off and the window being open probably offered him as much encouragement as he needed."

"What about the back of the house? I would think it more likely he would try to come in that way."

"Not with all the windows closed there. Just the same, I stationed Billy there with a gun of his own to keep an eye out for his coming. Anyway, I heard his boots crossing the gravel from the bunkhouse long before he reached the house. From the window corner I saw him keep to the shadows as he skulked along the wall. I knew he was coming on an errand of death. It was just a matter of getting him before he got me. He was just in the act of opening the window to creep in, when I flung open the door and let him have a bellyful from my shotgun. He spun from it and hit the dirt face-first. I left him where he was to go out back to the shed for a shovel. Billy's back there now digging the hole."

"You were planning on burying him without reporting it to the marshal?"

"You ever met the marshal?"

"No, but I've heard about him."

"Then you'll probably have heard that he owes his allegiance to Tull Clancy and not to the inhabitants of the town and its environs. If this is one of his men— and I think we can assume it is— then it'll bring nothing but trouble if he's found dead here."

"That you and Billy are safe and sound is all that matters," said Simona, entwining her arm in his at his side.

Nettle, who disliked being the object of anyone's concern, however well intentioned, looked from his daughter to Hornet with an uncomfortable smile. "How's Charlie Sykes, by the way? Were you able to learn anything?"

"No. He's dead. A Clancy man got to him before we reached his cabin. They burned it down, and we found his blackened body inside. However, we also discovered three bullet holes in his back, so we're certain the fire was started to make it look like an accident."

A shadow passed over Nettle's face. "Those are grim tidings. Somebody ought to gather all the citizens who are tired of the Clancys and converge on their ranch house and drive them out."

"Are you suggesting that you're the man to do that?"

"Maybe I am."

"It would involve going up against not only the Clancys and their gunmen but probably also the marshal."

"The marshal's no real lawman."

"Listen to you two," said Simona, perturbed by what she was hearing. "Why do you want to look for trouble like that?"

"It seems to me that the trouble's already come to us," replied Hornet.

"Simona, why don't you put on fresh coffee for us? I'd like to talk this over with John."

"I can see that a woman's opinion doesn't count for much when it comes to dealing death and destruction against your neighbors," snorted Simona as she headed into the house.

When she'd gone, Hornet resumed the conversation. "You mean what you said about maybe going up against the Clancys?"

"I do— if there were enough of us."

Hornet nodded in agreement and gave the older

man free rein to put his evolving ideas into words.

"I guess if everyone we knew and a few others beside put in with us, we would have enough. I don't doubt that when folks hear about what happened to Sykes and the attack here as well as the suspicions related to your father's death, public sentiment might be strongly on our side."

"Before the night is out, there might be two more deaths," said Hornet, sounding a grim note.

"Who do you mean?"

"Whoever the other two signers to the contract are. Wish I knew who they were."

"Whoever turns up dead is who it is," said Nettle, sounding an even grimmer note.

"Mr. Nettle, what about rounding up everyone you know for a meeting on the subject?"

Nettle scratched at his sideburn. "That's a good idea, son. I think I might do that. It's late now, but I'll see to it tomorrow."

"I don't feel like I have too many friends left in these parts, but I'll do my part and try to encourage those I know to attend the meeting. Where's it to be?"

"Maybe at Charlie Sykes's cabin— or what's left of it. Then people can see what we're up against."

"Good thinking. But we'll have to be careful who we trust. If someone were to inform the Clancys, they might be waiting outside the cabin ruins to give us a warm reception."

"Anyone who's close to any of the lawmen should be left out of this."

"That new deputy can probably be trusted. He's already helped me out once. That reminds me. There's a tree outside town where he promised to leave messages if any useful information came his way. I think I'll head out to it first thing in the morning and see if he's left me something."

◆ ◆ ◆

Hornet fell asleep within seconds of his head touching the pillow of the bed in the Nettles' guest room, and was awake again before dawn. His intention was to eat his breakfast in the saddle on the way to his destination. He also had a supply of jerky, biscuits and dried fruit should he be away longer.

When he went out to the barn for his horse, Simona was waiting for him.

"I've heard it said before that I cling to people I care about like a vine," she said, petting his horse. "Do you think it's true?"

"You look beautiful first thing in the morning."

"You're evading the question, but thank you for the compliment. I wouldn't mind it at all if you bestowed them more often."

"Does this mean that you intend to come with me?"

"No. I know enough to know that I might be in the way, wherever it is you're going. I'm just here to say goodbye."

Hornet took her in his arms and held her tight as they kissed.

"Some men find that being with a clinger can be

inconvenient and even insufferable," she whispered into his ear.

"Those men are fools."

With the warm taste of her lips still on his own, Hornet rode out. Like the sweetheart or wife of every soldier who ever went off to battle, she reminded him to be careful.

Later that morning he reached the oak tree at the crossroads outside of town. He wasn't expecting a message of much relevance, so he was elated when he found one:

Hornet,

Hopefully you will read this in time. I thought you might like to know the Clancys are now in possession of both maps. The two eldest Clancy brothers, William and Edward, plan to ride out in search of the gold. This will be Wednesday morning, the 3rd of April, at sun-up. Nobody outside of the Clancys knows where the final destination is. All that is known is they will be heading north through the mountain pass, somewhere beyond which they'll dig it up. They will then continue to the mining town of Hope's End and deposit the gold with the bank there. I know all this because Marshal Briscot, Deputy Fairhaven, myself and three or four Clancy gunhands have been instructed to guard the pass in the event that you or anyone else tries to follow them.

I don't have to tell you that you'll be arrested if you attempt to go through that pass, although it's more likely you'll be shot on sight.

If you intend to pursue the Clancys, your only hope is to make your way over the mountain ahead of

them. Circumventing it would take too long.
Godspeed.

T. Dugan

Hornet, after reading it through twice, lit a match to the message and watched it curl up into ashes on the ground. It was certainly very useful information. Today was Wednesday, the day that the Clancys planned to set out to retrieve the chest. He looked at the horizon, where the sun was just beginning to break. His enemies were perhaps a few miles closer to the pass than he was at the moment, but there might still be time to cross the mountain ahead of them, especially if they had not yet set out.

Hornet, having made his decision, rode for the pass. Knowing it would be folly to use the northern road, he instead headed up a rarely used rough track that cut through the great expanse of wide-open country stretching toward the northern mountain that was his destination. His horse was far from fresh, and probably the same could be said about himself. But with a bit of luck and if he didn't push his horse too hard, he felt he could reach the pass before the Clancys.

As the miles sped past, the darkness of the land was lifted to reveal the rolling, undulating prairie he was passing through like a ship making its way through the waters of the sea. Ahead, surmounted by bands of red and gold against a clear blue morning sky that had been unveiled, were the serrated peaks he was bound for. This — everywhere, all around him— was the land that he had known and loved since childhood. He knew now that he was wrong to ever have left it. Here he would stay and fight for his future, whatever that might be. Life was hard, it was true, but he would never again allow himself to be driven away by his enemies.

Hornet was in the densely wooded foothills leading to the mountain, when he heard the rumble of a wagon and the pounding hoofs of maybe ten riders in a file. They were coming up the winding path that joined his farther ahead, and beyond which was the long sloping final approach to the pass containing few trees. He was actually a little ahead of them, but if he dashed ahead now, he'd come into view and be picked off.

There was nothing to be done now but to keep out of sight behind the screen of trees and watch them pass.

An idea came to him, fraught with risk as it was.

Seeing no other recourse, he put his idea into action. When the last rider had passed, he fell in behind him. Hopefully in the half-light and with the riders being sleepy and unalert, he would be taken for one of them.

Not long thereafter, the column began entering the pass. This was where the greatest danger lay. Hornet dreaded the thought of everyone gathering in the pass to receive final instructions, whereupon he might come to their attention and be exposed.

It was with great relief that he noticed the two foremost riders, whom he presumed were the Clancy brothers, and the wagon continue on with hardly a backward glance. Even better, the remaining riders ahead of him one by one dismounted and, leading their horses, fanned out across the face of the mountain to take up their positions.

He wasn't sure, but he thought he recognized the deputy among them. His eye returned to the wagon. Until now it had escaped his attention that there was someone sitting alongside the wagon driver. The passenger, whoever he was, was wrapped in a hooded cloak, perhaps against the cold or sun, as if old or feeble. In all probability, it was Tull Clancy himself. There'd been rumors that he'd been in ill health and hadn't been seen out of doors for several weeks. But whether Clancy was sick or not, it still meant an extra gun to contend with.

When Hornet reached the point where the others before him had dismounted, he rode just a little farther than any of the others before himself dismounting. Up ahead he could see that the Clancy brothers and wagon were still in sight. Operating under the assumption that he might be seen by some of those behind him, he then headed up one of the timbered slopes to the side. Once he was in amongst the timber shielded from view, he threaded his way through conifers and pine trees on a course parallel to the trail that ran on in a jagged pattern. Here the sweet scent of early mountain flowers and the resinous tang of unending trees carried on the breeze.

It was slow going, particularly where there were fallen trees, but worth the effort to remain out of sight from both directions. When those he pursued rounded the first bend and he followed suit, he had nothing further to worry about with regard to the men behind him. Thereafter, a series of switchbacks and hairpin turns as well as the dense growth of timber kept him out of sight of the Clancys as well as the Clancys out of his sight ahead of him.

When it began to rain, he got out his slicker. When it changed to a hailfall, he stopped under a tree to avoid being pelted by hail the size of potatoes. After some minutes, it slackened again to rain. He wondered whether the Clancys had also stopped and thought it likely. Foolishly he had dismounted under the tree instead of sitting his horse, which resulted in the discomfort of sitting in a wet saddle when he got underway again.

Once out of the mountains, it proved easy to follow the twin ruts made by the wagon, enabling him to keep as far back as he liked. Through ravines, canyons and open flatlands, he stayed with them in the days that followed. Only occasionally did he sight them in the distance. When they bedded down for the night, he did as well, but still at a distance. It was easy to know when they had stopped. Not suspecting that anyone was pursuing them, they always built a fire for cooking and for warmth, which could be seen for miles off. Hornet built his own fire each night, but always sheltered behind a ridge, bluff or boulders and using deadwood, which gave off almost no smoke. One morning, when he'd awoken under a bluff, he found five or six old chipped arrowheads in the shale, an indication that where he'd lain might have been the scene of some ancient battle.

He passed through countless streams and marshes that were full of beaver-dams constructed out of mud and sticks. Occasionally when crossing streams his horse faltered as it tried to find its footing on the slippery, pebble-strewn ground bordering the water, just as he could see that those ahead of him he was following sometimes had as well. There were wild geese and other animals in abundance, many of them so tame that they thought nothing of coming almost within his reach.

Once, about three days out, he noticed that the Clancys had stopped to gather around the wagon. After some moments of studying them from afar, he realized the wagon had broken down and that they were mending a wheel or axle. Hornet withdrew behind the shadow of a ridge, where, reclining in a comfortable bed of buffalo grass and moss, he had a smoke and waited. After two or three hours, with the problem fixed, they moved on again.

On the fourth day, they entered a high-walled canyon with no way out except through the entrance. Could this at long last, Hornet wondered, be where the chest was buried? Very deliberately they went to the far end of the canyon, and there, about a hundred feet from the sheer granite wall, they began digging. Only the passenger in the wagon that he assumed was Tull Clancy remained where he was, apart from the others. William, Edward and the driver were all excitedly focusing their attention on their task of digging up the treasure. True to the imperious and high-handed nature of the brothers, it was perhaps no surprise that it was the driver who was doing all the digging, observed Hornet.

From the cover of a cluster of boulders just inside the canyon entrance, Hornet observed them. He was as eager as anyone to catch the first glittering sight of the gold.

One thing troubled him. How was he going to prevent four armed and highly motivated men from making off with the gold?

Chapter Fifteen

Even before he caught sight of the chest, Hornet knew they'd found it from the way the Clancys were celebrating. The back of one of them was to him, but the sound of his gunfire told him that they were blasting open the lock.

With the lock sprung, the lid was heaved back. Hands instinctively dipped into the gold nuggets and held them up high. It was then that Hornet caught his first sparkling glimpse and wet his lips. An echo that sounded like "Enough to rule the world!" echoed to his end of the canyon.

A rage gripped Hornet as he thought of how half the treasure rightly belonged to his sister and, because he knew she would share it, to himself. Few things in life were worth dying for, but with all his soul he felt that this was one of them. He had no idea what the precise value was, but he reckoned that just a fraction of it would help to rebuild the Hornet ranch and buy new stock, take on new hands and restore his family's honor.

The chest, he now saw, was lifted up out of the hole and loaded onto the back of the wagon. They would soon be leaving. Hornet withdrew to where he'd left his horse outside the mouth of the canyon. Climbing into the saddle, he rode off.

◆ ◆ ◆

Not long after, the Clancys with their wagon were passing through a narrow defile on their way to Hope's End.

"Hold it right there!" commanded Hornet, getting to his feet so he could be seen. "You're covered on both sides. Anyone that moves is a dead man."

The reaction was about what he would have expected. All faces turned to Hornet on the cliff wall pointing the gleaming barrel of his rifle down at them. There was a startled gasp which came from the cloaked figure. The foremost Clancy, William, pulled up hard and circled once before looking from Hornet to another man who loomed across from him on the opposite wall in a shadowy nest of boulders. This ally of Hornet's was in actuality a dummy propped up by a log and sticks and clothed in his jacket, bandana and his hat pulled low. A filling of leaves inside the sleeves helped to give the arms the appearance of depth. Yet in the shadows the prop looked enough like an armed human to be taken seriously at that moment by the Clancys.

William Clancy was more angry than surprised at Hornet being there. "How could you be here, Hornet? It's not possible, damn you. You couldn't have slipped through the pass. I had five or six men guarding it. Was it in the dark you got through?"

"Though you never guessed it, I came right along with you. You should have looked back at the last man following you."

"What an annoying little cockroach you turned out to be."

"You can oblige me by throwing down your side-arms now— all of you," said Hornet with a threatening sweep of his muzzle before it settled again on William Clancy.

"First," said Clancy, "I'd like you to get a look at my bride-to-be. We're to be married in Hope's End later today." Maneuvering his horse closer to the wagon's passenger, Clancy threw back the hood.

"Hattie!" cried Hornet, who'd assumed all this time that his sister was in hiding. The Clancys must have rooted her out or else intercepted her on the way to the valley.

Startled by the sight of his sister and not wishing to point his rifle in her direction, Hornet instinctively lowered his weapon. This was all the opening that his three adversaries needed.

"John, watch out!"

The driver, digging his revolver out of his holster, fired at Hornet, missed clean and was in the process of lining up another shot, when Hornet, having recovered from his initial shock, dropped to one knee. Aligning his sights, he sent a bullet into the driver's chest, which toppled him from the wagon.

Having left their driver to deal with Hornet, both Clancys opened fire on the dummy, hitting it several times before it collapsed in a heap, at which point they realized it was no human target.

Hattie meanwhile screamed as the two wagon horses, terrified by the gunfire, reared, then bolted, taking her and the treasure chest with them. The pack-mules brayed and were pulled along behind. Unable to get out of the way in time as his own horse reared out of control, Ed Clancy was bowled over by the rampaging horses and fell from his saddle. When he hit the ground, his head split open on a rock, sending a spray of blood into the gravel.

Hornet, pinned down by the deadly return fire of the remaining Clancy, kept his head low behind a bulge in the rimrock as the probing bullets sent up a shower of rock fragments. Seeing the horses run off, William Clancy fired a parting shot at Hornet, wheeled and tore off in pursuit of the runaway wagon.

By the time Hornet raised his head again, Clancy was almost at the end of the defile about to break into open ground. Hornet quickly scrambled up the rocks behind him and then onto the plateau where he'd hobbled his horse. It took a couple of precious minutes to get down off the plateau and then out into the open. By then, the others were a half mile ahead of him.

Putting spurs to his sorrel, he forged ahead at a dead run over the track.

Two miles distant, Hornet came to the rim of a vast basin fringed with conifers and shrubs. Before him were dozens of larger and smaller pools of water. Some were of clear, pristine water; others were cloudy with mud. Still others contained acidic boiling waters from which steam arose. Here and there were geysers continually sputtering. At irregular intervals a great thundering roar could be heard as one of them erupted, sending a column of hot water and steam gushing up into the air. All about were billowing masses of smoke drifting over both land and water as if from artillery batteries deployed on a field of battle, and ever present was the noxious stench of sulphur. Here and there were leafless lodgepole pine trees, their trunks blanched and protruding out of the earth at odd angles, suggesting upheavals from below ground.

Hornet had heard of this wild, desolate place but had forgotten its name, if it even had one. An old trapper he once spoke to up on the balcony of a hotel front had said that hell itself could be found just below the surface here.

There, a quarter-mile into the basin at the edge of a churning hot spring was the wagon. Hattie lay in the back, her hair tousled and her arm bruised but otherwise unhurt. The horses, having broken loose from their harness, were nowhere to be seen. One of the two pack-mules, however, was still there. Clancy was in the process of transferring the gold from the chest into the packsaddles of the mule. When he saw Hornet approaching, he stopped what he was doing and fired a bullet in his direction.

Hornet, however, veered his horse behind the nearest rise, where he left it tied to a scrubby bush. As soon as he'd pulled his rifle from its scabbard lined with fleece, he decided then and there that he would be both brave and reckless this day and that that was the only way to save his sister. Throwing caution to the wind, he made a zigzagging dash on foot to another rise and then another even as the bullets went flying past.

With his enemy unharmed and getting close, Clancy clambered up into the wagon and put Hattie between him and her brother.

"Let my sister go, Clancy. Let her go, and you can keep the gold."

"I want both, Hornet."

Hornet, now thirty paces away and partly shielded by a pine tree, said nothing to this.

"Where's my brother?"

"Lying back there."

"You shoot him?"

"No. Hit himself on the head when he fell— got knocked unconscious," lied Hornet, fearful that the truth might prompt Clancy to take out his grief and anger on Hattie.

"You've caused me a lot of trouble."

"You've caused me and Hattie even more."

Clancy laughed. "Maybe you're right about that, if I have to be honest. But to achieve greatness in this life, a man must be both daring and ruthless. These are the qualities that have formed the bedrock of every prominent, moneyed family and empire that ever existed. That's something you could never understand in a thousand years."

"And how many of those greats repented of their earthly sins on their death bed?"

"Bah. Very few, I'll wager. Repentance is for the weak of mind. But listen. How about the following idea. You go back and revive my brother and bring him to me. Then we'll talk some more."

"I don't think much of your idea."

"You don't have to." There was a pause as Clancy's thoughts wandered to an unrelated subject. "Say, Johnny:

remember when me and you used to go fly-fishing as youngsters? Those were the days. You won't believe it, but there are times when I actually feel a sentimental yearning for the simplicity and innocence of those days."

"Why'd you kill Charlie Sykes?"

"I don't admit to that, and if I did, why should I tell you anything?"

"You know my word and Hattie's word against yours wouldn't be enough to see justice done."

"True enough. All right, then. I'll tell you. He died because of what he knew."

"You mean because he was one of the signers of that contract between our fathers?"

"That's right."

"But even if you killed everyone that knew about the agreement, what would it get you? Copies of the contract itself would still exist."

"My original inclination was to erase all trace of the contracts and anything else related to the agreement our fathers signed, including the witnesses. But when I got to thinking about the risks involved should you someday show up with that document you stole, even it being just a copy, I changed my mind. Also, I learned that your father's old lawyer, Samuel Puttman, now lives outside the territory, somewhere unknown at present, which meant that it would take time to track him down, if he could be found at all. I feared he too might one day turn up with his own draft of the contract. So rather than pursue a bloody and clumsy course, I decided it was best to solidify my position through marriage to Hattie."

"So before you saw fit to change your strategy, all it cost was the life of Sykes and whatever other witnesses you were able to get to."

"Sykes was the only one. We made a try for Nathan Nettle, but he escaped his fate, which I have a feeling you already know about."

"Aren't you forgetting my old man?"

"I didn't have anything to do with that."

"It was your father behind it, then?"

"That's his own affair."

"So I take it your father took possession of our half of the map just before killing my father?"

Clancy was about to answer. Then, thinking better of it, he gave a non-committal shrug, which, to Hornet, was as good as an admission of his father's guilt.

"But if that's so, why'd you wait this long to go after the gold?"

"We couldn't at that time."

"What do you mean?"

"We couldn't for the very simple reason that we didn't have our half of the map. We only had yours."

Hornet blinked. "What? How's that possible? What happened to your half?"

"Never mind. It... went missing for a time. Anyway, you were of tremendous help to us, though you didn't realize it, when you pilfered my father's desk at his office in town the other day. When we saw the secret compartment you'd uncovered, we worked out what you must have found. Though we didn't know at the time that it'd just been a copy, we decided to look in my father's matching desk back at the ranch, and, sure enough, we found our half of the map hidden there in original form."

"But why didn't your father just tell you where it was?"

"He's been ill of late, you jackass."

"But surely not that ill that he couldn't tell you

where to look."

"Like I said, it went missing. As for my father, he's all right," snarled Clancy. "He'll be fine. He's on his way to a full recovery, which is a sight better than can be said about your father."

"You're a devil, Clancy— you and your old man."

Clancy pressed the muzzle of his gun against Hattie's cheek, causing her to cry out in anguish. "You just do as I say, Hornet, or I'll make myself a widower-man even afore I can become a bridegroom."

"You said a moment ago you needed Hattie to marry her; now you say you want to kill her?"

"I'm a complex man prone to making quick changes in plans as circumstances evolve. Here's another change. I want you to drop your rifle on the ground right there at your feet."

Hornet's eyes narrowed.

Clancy cocked his gun. "You going to do like I ask?" he said, pressing the nozzle still harder against Hattie's cheek.

Hattie, crying out again, began to sob.

Hornet's mind cleared. There was something he'd forgotten which he now remembered. "Hattie," he said, addressing his sister, "don't worry; we'll get out of this. Keep in mind that there's always hope."

"Except when there's not," snickered Clancy.

"Hattie," he continued, "do you remember when I found you at Mrs. Brockbane's establishment and instilled hope in you. In a way, it passed from her to you. She had it and then lost it to you. Now you have it. Hattie, I think you should use that hope right now. With hope you can overcome anything— even William— assuming you still have it."

"You're both religious zealots, I see. But hope and faith won't do either of you any good when confronted by cold, hard steel," sneered Clancy.

"Johnny..." said Hattie, understanding at last; "I want you to know I still have hope."

Hornet smiled. "Good, Hattie. I'm glad to hear it." Then, to Clancy he added, "I'm going to put my rifle down now."

Clancy watched him closely— so closely that he didn't pay any attention to his hostage. With her nimble fingers Hattie undid the clasp of her reticule and probed the contents until her fingers alighted on the pearl handle of Mrs. Brockbane's Derringer. Her thumb fell upon the hammer. Once, years ago, she'd fired a similar gun. She slowly brought the hammer back, then lifted the gun out of the reticule.

Hornet was putting his rifle gently down onto the ground. Clancy, having watched with eager eyes, began to direct the muzzle of his gun away from Hattie's face and toward her brother. That was when Hattie made a swift motion with her hand. To Clancy in that brief moment he thought he glimpsed the movement of a dove's wing. The muzzle of the Derringer thumped against his upper chest as Hattie pulled the trigger. Suddenly there was a loud crash as the bullet drove in through his chest and out his shoulder, releasing a jet of blood in its wake.

Clancy's body bucked from the impact. With Clancy's grip loosening on his revolver, Hornet lunged at him.

"Oh, God! God!" cried Hattie, her body convulsing with fear and horror at what she had done. She retched over the right side of the wagon and then scrambled over that same side to the ground in order to get away from

Clancy and what she had done.

Meanwhile, Hornet, having succeeded in twisting Clancy's gun out of his hand, threw it as far as he could from the wagon. But Clancy wasn't finished. Despite the wound high in his chest, there was still fight in him. Consumed by rage and pain, he bared his teeth like a trapped wolf and even snarled like one. With unexpected speed given his condition, Clancy pounded his fist into Hornet's face, driving him back. Hornet, shaking off the blow, answered with a hard uppercut of his own that sent Clancy reeling over the left side of the wagon and tumbling down the bank into the pool of seething acid water there.

Clancy shrieked like a madman as he came to the surface. He thrashed about in agony as he attempted to make it back to the margin of the pool.

Hornet, retrieving his rifle, rushed out onto a half-submerged outcrop at the pool's edge and held the weapon out by the barrel for Clancy to take hold of the stock. "Grab hold! Grab hold, Willy!"

But disoriented and blinded from the acidic water, he was unable to connect with the stock.

Hornet tapped the end against Clancy's knuckles to show him where it was, but a frantic groping didn't result in Clancy taking hold of it.

Hattie, too, tried her best to save her friend of old, gathering up a dead branch and pushing it out toward him. "Willy! Willy! Take hold! No— more to your right!" she cried.

"Hattieeeee!" he wailed pitifully as he recognized her voice. But this branch, too, he failed to connect with.

A fresh wave of extreme pain shot through Clancy. His body convulsed with agony as he twisted away from the stock and branch that might have been his salvation. Still thrashing about but weakening, he swam farther out into the water away from the shore.

"No! This way! This way, Willy!" shouted Hornet.

But by this time it was too late. Clancy unleashed one long, final, desperate shriek that was like the sound of a soul being torn from its body. Soon he all but stopped struggling as he drifted away. A low pitiful whimpering hung in the air a few moments longer, then a gurgling as the mouth went below the surface. One of Clancy's hands lingered for a while above the water, twitching slightly before disappearing forever.

Concentric ripples marked his passage; then there was nothing. The acid water had taken him, and William Clancy was no more. In a few hours only his bleached bones would remain, and after some days even the bones would dissolve.

Racked with guilt and feeling terrified at what she had just witnessed, Hattie sought comfort in her brother's arms as she sobbed uncontrollably.

"It's over now," he whispered. "And our old friend is at peace."

Chapter Sixteen

Afraid that some of Clancy's men might still be guarding the mountain pass, Hornet first went through it alone. He needn't have worried. The men that had been there were long gone. Raising his rifle skyward, he fired off two rounds, which was the signal to his sister that all was well and that she could proceed. Minutes later she drew up alongside him on William Clancy's horse. Attached by a lead rope to her saddle was the trailing pack-mule laden with gold.

"Will it be safe for us to return?" asked Hattie.

"Look," said her brother, pointing to the smoke curling skyward in the distance. "I think that means it is."

Hattie stared at the rising smoke. "The Clancy ranch? It's coming from there?"

"Yes. It looks like Nathan Nettle delivered on his promise. He vowed to rally every able-bodied man he could to drive out the Clancys, and I think that's what he did."

"It's strange to think that the Clancys might not be a threat to us any longer."

"Well, there might be a few remaining renegades around that we'll have to watch out for, but I think the power of the Clancys might be broken forever."

The brother and sister descended from the mountain into the lowlands and crossed the forest that then led to the open ranges. At last they stood before the Triangle X.

They looked upon a scene of desolation. The battle between the Clancys and Nettle's forces had long since ended, but several haystacks and outbuildings still smouldered and a dozen bodies still lay where they had fallen. The corrals were all empty of their horses.

Surprisingly, much of the main house still stood, though its east and west wings were burnt and pitted. For some reason the fires started at the ends had not taken hold in the central part of the house.

The score of townspeople and valley settlers wandering or standing about assured Hornet and his sister that the Clancy ranch was in the hands of its enemies. There were also two or three women or sweethearts grieving over the bodies of their slain men.

Nettle and Deputy Dugan stepped out into view from behind the house just then.

"I'm glad to see you two are safe," said Nettle.

"And I'm glad to be able to say the same about you two," replied Hornet, climbing down from his horse and shaking hands with Nettle and Dugan. "It looks like you had quite a battle on your hands." He looked at the deputy. "In particular, I'd like to thank you for that message you left me, Deputy, though I didn't think to see you join the battle against the Clancys."

"I felt, as a lawman, I should be present to offer them a chance to surrender. That's not the way they wanted it, so we opened fire on those who chose to resist."

"What about the marshal? I'm surprised he didn't try to get in your way. It seems to me like he's almost one of them."

"He *was* one of them. That's him lying over there," said the deputy, pointing to a twisted body lying face down and half-obscured by the trunk of a cottonwood. "He said that I had no authority here and we'd be the ones to be arrested if we didn't go peaceably on our way. Well, we didn't go away, and the marshal was one of the first to be killed."

"Wasn't there another deputy?"

"Fairhaven? Yeah, but he decided to stay out of it. He's still in town."

"I know that the Clancys employed a lot of hands, including at least a dozen hired guns. Are they all accounted for?"

"Most of the hired guns were killed. Some run off. A lot of the regular hands either surrendered or run off too. Four of the hard cases, including Jake Malloy, made a stand over by a corral shed. They all perished there except for one wounded man who's expected to live. We got all the surrendered men held prisoner in the bunkhouse."

"I'm not surprised that Malloy put up the most resistance."

"Well, he had to. He knew he'd be strung up if he were taken alive. He and his gunmen had been running amok the past few days. It was the final prompting that those who were undecided needed to organize against them and finally attack the ranch."

"What about Mr. Clancy?"

"Tull Clancy? He's there in the house."

"You mean he's dead?"

"No."

"But aren't you going to arrest him?"

"Maybe you'd better go inside and see him for yourself. Then you'll understand why we didn't arrest him."

Hornet, slipping his rifle out of its scabbard, stalked past the deputy and Nettle.

"You won't need that," said Dugan. "There isn't any threat from anybody left alive in there now."

Hornet nonetheless held on to his rifle, keeping it level before him at hip level as he proceeded toward the house. Stepping past the bodies of the marshal and two other men, he mounted the steps leading to the colonnaded porch.

The twin doors ahead lay shattered and blackened as though they'd been opened with explosives. Here he found a body lying across the threshold and, beyond that, still another lay at the bottom of the staircase, a gun just beyond reach of one of the lifeless hands as if he'd died while trying to reach it. Looking at the face, Hornet saw that it was Earl, the youngest Clancy brother. The sight saddened him: firstly, because of his age —he wasn't more than seventeen— and also because he was well liked and gentle of nature. Hornet could hardly recall a time when he wasn't smiling, usually from the sheer joy of being alive.

Moving past Earl Clancy, he mounted the staircase. There was no sign of life in the house and his footsteps seemed to cause an unnaturally loud creaking in the silence. He suddenly felt like an unwelcome intruder. At the top of the stairs to the right was the half-opened door to Telford Clancy's inner sanctum at the back of the house. He'd only been in this room once in his life, many years ago, and he remembered how strong of an impression he was left with of the room corresponding exactly to the character of the man.

He pushed the door open with the barrel of his rifle. Despite what the deputy had said, he wasn't taking any chances. Even if Clancy had surrendered earlier and might have appeared as meek as a fawn, he might have subsequently had a change of heart and be bent on revenge, especially when he saw who he was. Why Clancy wasn't under arrest and already in or on his way to the holding cell in town puzzled him.

Slouched in an armchair by the window, just beyond the desk, was a figure, his back to Hornet.

The sound of a creak on the floorboard under Hornet's feet prompted the turning of the person's head.

"Clancy!"

Hornet heard a quick intake of breath, followed by a gurgling gasp. Clancy's glassy eyes were fixed on him. There were dark circles under his eyes. There was something else too. There was cold fear.

"I never took you for a coward. Stand up." Again there was a gurgle, but no movement to get up. "I said stand up and face me!"

"He couldn't stand up even if he wanted to," said a soft voice behind Hornet.

Hornet whirled. Standing in the doorway was Clancy's daughter, Anne.

"What do you mean he can't stand up?"

She crossed the room and positioned herself behind her father. "Didn't you notice? He's in a wheelchair," she said as she turned the wheelchair toward Hornet so that her father faced him.

Clancy, spittle dripping from the edge of his mouth, was struggling to speak. He gasped and wheezed, then seemed to give up before retracting his neck and head into his hunched shoulders like a frightened turtle. Most pathetic of all were the haunted eyes darting from Hornet to one side or the other of the room as though Clancy found the world a terrifying place.

"Does he even recognize me?"

"Who can tell?"

"What happened to him?"

"He had a stroke or seizure about three weeks ago when he was out riding. The fall made it all the worse when he struck his head. He hasn't spoken a coherent word since then."

"Three weeks ago? But who's been running everything all this time? Who's been organizing gunmen to hunt me and my sister down? Who put Hattie in a house of ill repute?"

"It was my father who was behind the decision to do what was done to your sister. Everything done up to three weeks ago was his doing. After that, it was William who issued orders and ran things in his name. It's been him ever since."

"Why was his illness kept a secret?"

"We decided early on, as soon as it was apparent that he was unlikely to recover, that we wouldn't let anyone know what sort of state he was in."

"But why? What was the point of hiding his condition?"

"Pride, for one thing. I know my father well enough to know that he'd rather have died than be seen as he is. Also, it takes a strong hand to run this ranch and our other business concerns and to keep everything together. It was through strength and the power of his reputation that he built it up. So it was to our advantage that everyone continue to believe my father was still in control and making the decisions, even if he was out of sight."

"I suppose you also still held out hope he might one day recover."

"Yes, though it's very unlikely. But now that everyone has finally seen him as he is —as a shell of what he once was—" Anne left her sentence unfinished.

"What will you do with him now?"

"It's become impossible for us to stay here. In a day or two we'll pack up our belongings in a wagon and head to St. Louis, where my aunt owns a cottage. He'll live out the remainder of his days there, though in greatly diminished circumstances."

"But surely you're still well-fixed?"

Anne hesitated a moment, then decided there was no point in keeping to herself what was about to become public knowledge. "Everything we have will soon be gone. There's already been talk of reparations and the seizure of all assets. We'll probably fight them in court, but with public sentiment the way it is, the case is likely to go against us."

"Wait here a minute. I want to give you something before I leave, assuming I can get my sister's approval."

Hornet went back outside. After conferring with his sister and getting her consent for what he had in mind, he returned with a packsaddle, which he lay on the floor next to where Anne Clancy still stood.

"What's that?" she asked.

Hornet lifted back the flap, which revealed raw nuggets of gold. "This is about a fifth of the total. By rights, you should get half, but, considering everything that's been done to us, I think it's only fair we keep the lion's share."

"Does this mean that William and Eddy are dead?"

"They gave me no choice. I'm sorry."

Anne nodded almost imperceptibly as a tear trickled from her eye in memory of her brothers.

"I only have one condition," said Hornet.

"What's that?"

"That you and everyone else from this ranch never show yourselves in these parts again." He reflected a moment before offering a concession. "I'm not talking about those in your employ who are honest and took no part in the fighting, but everyone else."

Anne having agreed to this condition, Hornet went outside again to rejoin his sister.

"Where shall we go now?" asked Hattie. "The hotel?"

"I've got somewhere else in mind," replied her brother, mounting his horse. "We've got a standing invitation to stay with Simona and her father for as long as we like."

"I've always liked her."

Hornet turned and smiled at his sister next to him as they rode out. "I think she's always liked you too, Hattie. And she'll like you even better as a sister-in-law."

~END~

The U.S. Marshal Flint series:

Trailed
Blood Feud
Vengeance

The Johnny Hornet series:

The Long Arm of Tull Clancy
Assassins on the Loose
Final Stand

Manufactured by Amazon.ca
Acheson, AB

16220748R00094